IVY COMPTO

THE MIGHTY
AND THEIR FALL

WITH A NEW INTRODUCTION BY
HILARY SPURLING

Published by VIRAGO PRESS Limited 1990
20–23 Mandela Street, Camden Town, London NW1 0HQ

First published in Great Britain by Victor Gollancz 1955
Copyright Ivy Compton-Burnett 1955
Introduction Copyright © Hilary Spurling 1990

A CIP catalogue record for this book is available from the British Library

Printed in Great Britain by Cox & Wyman Ltd, Reading, Berks

INTRODUCTION

Ivy Compton-Burnett is a puzzle. She was born in 1884, within a year or so of Virginia Woolf, James Joyce and D.H. Lawrence, but her particular originality could hardly be further from the strenuous pioneering effort, the stylistic shock tactics and underlying romanticism of the giants of the Modern Movement. Her tone is cool, dry, sharp, irreverent and ironic. She was over forty when she made her debut in the 1920s alongside a much younger generation of novelists like Evelyn Waugh and Anthony Powell, with whom she had in some ways more in common than with her own contemporaries, whose imaginations had been formed and furnished before the First World War.

Pastors and Masters appeared in 1925. "It is astonishing, amazing. It is like nothing else in the world. It is a work of genius," wrote the *New Statesman*'s reviewer. Its wit, acidity and quiet cynicism were picked up at once in *Vogue* by the young Raymond Mortimer, who would be one of the first to recognise in the strange, condensed and abstracted forms of I. Compton-Burnett's early novels the closest it was possible to come to post-impressionism in fiction. For Mortimer and others like him between the wars, she represented the last word in bold and daring innovation: "something quite, quite new," said Rosamond Lehmann. "I was so dazzled by it, she became my favourite novelist immediately." If the young were enthusiastic, the literary establishment responded with understandable caution to works that seemed to embody all the more unwholesome, frivolous and unsettling tendencies of decadent modern youth. I. Compton-Burnett's second novel, which became something of an intellectual rallying point for bright young things in 1929, had been turned down in manuscript by Leonard Woolf at the Hogarth Press ("She can't even write," he said), and her growing reputation in avant-garde circles over the next decade continued to give his wife Virginia sleepless nights.

From the beginning Ivy's mystery strengthened her appeal. Nobody knew who she was or where she came from, and the few who met her were deeply disconcerted to find a nondescript, retiring, resolutely uncommunicative character who dressed and behaved more like a Victorian governess than a radical iconoclast. She had not yet evolved the protective formal carapace she would acquire in later life, when her austere features, erect carriage and penetrating stare often petrified even the most sophisticated observers. She seemed already formidably severe to Anthony Powell, when he met her for the first time after the second war. "Ivy Compton-Burnett embodied a quite unmodified pre-1914 personality," he wrote, identifying the extraordinary impression she produced in fact as a construct no less stylised and artificial than the Victorian settings of her fiction. "Her jewellery managed never to look like jewellery but, on her, seemed hieratic insignia," wrote the painter Robin Fedden, describing Ivy in her prime:

I do not recall seeing her out of black. She wore it like a uniform, with care but with the disregard of mode proper to uniform. A sense positively of the services attached to a black tricorne, vaguely reminiscent of an eighteenth-century quarter-deck . . . For me, the physical impression was recurrently of a Roman head, a soldier-emperor, perhaps Galba. The rolled hair and the ribbon sometimes seemed like a laurel wreath.

By the time she died in 1969 she had become a legend, a public image so forbidding and remote that, when I set out soon afterwards to write her life, I found it hard at first to credit the fond, sociable, disarmingly absurd and affectionate creature described by friends who sorely missed her. The discrepancy was only one of many contradictions about her life and work for, as Powell pointed out, the two could not be separated, nor could the mystery of the one be solved without recourse to the other. Again and again her admirers had found themselves baffled and brought up short by her sedate appearance and resolutely prim small talk. It was as if the Victorian trappings provided, in both fact and fiction, a protective cover behind which her penetrating subversive intelligence might operate unsuspected, freely and without constraint.

There was little Ivy did not know, and nothing she could not say, about the ravages of jealousy, lust, greed, vanity, cruelty and aggression: the physical and emotional abuses perpetrated behind a façade of eminently respectable domesticity in her books. Her plots may take place in the 1890s but her preoccupations belong unequivocally to the twentieth century. Politics did not detain her. She had no interest in radical or any other sort of chic, but she spent the better part of her life analysing steadily and with unnerving precision the totalitarian misuse of power in a closed society, the pollution of thought and language, the ruthless oppression by the strong of weak and vulnerable victims. "I write of power being destructive," Ivy said, when asked about the violence and repression inside her nineteenth-century families, "and parents had absolute power over children in those days. One or the other had." She set her books at the time of her own girlhood in a world smashed and obliterated by the 1914-18 war. Her own early life supplied a body of material which she used, not for subjective exploration, but to examine dispassionately, in a series of clinically controlled fictional experiments, the squalor and brutality as well as the courage, generosity and endurance secreted in the tenderest and most private recesses of the human heart.

Ivy was born in Pinner in 1884, the seventh child of a leading homeopathic physician, Dr James Compton-Burnett. She was the first child of his second marriage: her mother, Katharine Compton-Burnett, was a beautiful, delicate, imaginative, imperious and highly competitive woman who had met her future husband as his patient, and fallen passionately in love with him. Their devotion was mutual and, when Dr Burnett's first wife died in childbirth, he remarried so promptly that Ivy was born less than two years after her last half brother. Her mother inherited five small stepchildren (one had already died in infancy), ranging in age from eight years old down to the new baby, and over the next fifteen years she bore seven more of her own.

Dr Burnett installed his growing family for the sake of their health in a capacious house on the south coast at Hove, spending the greater part of each week himself away in town, immersed in the demands of a rapidly expanding London practice. Katharine Compton-Burnett, who was easily bored by domesticity and had never in any case cared for children, found herself immured without outside contacts or adult company in a household full of increasing numbers of her own and her hated predecessor's offspring. She possessed neither the inner resources nor the external support that might have helped her to bear loneliness and frustration. The children, competing for attention and affection in nursery and schoolroom, had no option but to submit to the steadily more tyrannical rule of an unchecked, unquestioned, unhappy and peremptory autocrat. It was a recipe for the kind of catastrophe which will be familiar enough to readers of I. Compton-Burnett.

Ivy herself grew up in a self-contained unit formed for mutual defence and protection with her beloved younger brothers, Guy and Noel. The three played together and shared a governess: Ivy, learning Latin and Greek with her brothers' tutor, was encouraged by the liberal and unorthodox Dr Burnett to prepare to read classics at London university (neither Oxford nor Cambridge gave degrees to women in those days). She had dearly loved her father, who died without warning from a heart attack in 1901 when she was sixteen. Her mother, hysterical and distraught, never fully recovered her mental or moral balance. She dressed the whole family in unrelieved black, retreating with them from now on to a life of almost complete isolation from the outside world, venting her depression on her eldest daughter and depending for consolation on Guy, who had always been her favourite. But Guy caught pneumonia and died as suddenly as his father in 1904, while Ivy was away in her final term at university. She had felt by her own account as close as a twin to Guy and now turned in her despair to Noel, forming an inseparable pair with him in the three years before he went up to Cambridge. The stepchildren had long since fled to London. Noel's departure left Ivy shut up at home with her mother, condemned to teach her four younger sisters, without friends of her own or openings or any imaginable prospect of escape. She had worn black throughout her youth in the long years of mourning for her father and Guy, and she wore it again in 1911 when Mrs Compton-Burnett died of cancer after a long and debilitating illness.

Under her mother's will, Ivy inherited the post of head of the household, establishing her own autocratic rule over her four sisters until they mutinied in 1915, and ran away together to set up an independent establishment in defiance of her authority in London. Noel had been for years Ivy's ally, her sole source of intellectual stimulation and emotional support in a decade of bitter desolation since Guy died. But Noel joined the army as a sub-lieutenant on the outbreak of war with Germany in August 1914, and was killed two years later in the battle of the Somme. Ivy could never talk afterwards about the war, nor speak of her brother to the day of her death without tears welling up in her eyes. The closing phase of the war marked the lowest point for the surviving Compton-Burnetts. Even Ivy, who had seemed rock-like, inscrutable, inured to grief and shock, could not withstand the blow which destroyed the last remnants of the only life she had ever known. No one had anticipated, or could ever afterwards explain, the deaths of her two youngest sisters who killed themselves, aged twenty-two and eighteen, by swallowing veronal behind the locked door of their bedroom on Christmas Day 1917.

Ivy fell ill after the inquest, and very nearly died herself in the deadly flu epidemic that swept London the following summer. She emerged slowly and painfully over the next few years from a period of prolonged mental, physical and emotional prostration, a state she described at the time as death in life. The publication of *Pastors and Masters* marked her recovery: a final distancing from the experiences of her first forty years which she never discussed in fact, but whose implications she would spend the next forty years and more exploring in fiction.

"People say that things don't happen like they do in my books," she once said earnestly to an old friend: *"Believe me, they do."* Her second novel, *Brothers and Sisters*, was of all her books the one that stuck most closely to her own past, examining the depradations of a jealous, demanding, extravagantly grief-stricken widow directly based on Ivy's mother. It is an unreassuring, if not unsympathetic portrait—one of the things Ivy's admirers found most disconcering was her refusal to dismiss or condemn her fictional tyrants out of hand—and it lays down for the first time a relationship with the past that would remain constant in all her subsequent novels. Sophia Stace stands revealed with disturbing clarity in the light of the hard, frank, unblinking stare Ivy's contemporaries found so essentially modern. "One suddenly sees that she is all that is worst in the nineteenth century," wrote a perceptive reviewer, comparing I. Compton-Burnett favourably with William Faulkner in the New York *Saturday Review* in 1929,

and the young people with their forthrightness and independence, all that is best of the twentieth. Their modernity gives them . . . the ability to go through the fire and escape the burning. All other books on this theme are stories of the present defeated by the past; *Brothers and Sisters* is a story of the present hurt by the past, but not defeated.

Ivy had tried once before to deal with much the same autobiographical material in *Dolores*, a solemn, agonised and thoroughly conventional account of the plight of a dutiful daughter at home, published in 1911 and afterwards disowned by its author, who made a point of turning its theme of self-sacrifice and self-repression upside down in all subsequent books. "The sight of duty does make one shiver," as somebody says in *Pastors and Masters*. "The actual doing of it would kill one, I think." The flippancy and high spirits of Ivy's early novels made them peculiarly provoking to readers who found her uncompromising truthfulness hard to take. Moral indignation added zest to her critics' more self-righteous stylistic objections, as Raymond Mortimer pointed out in 1935:

At first sight her work strikes you as clumsy and heavy-fisted; her figures, though solid, are not what is called "life-like", and she composes her books on highly defined and artificial designs. In fact, she is open to all the reproaches laid upon the founders of post-impressionism. And it is still as useless, I think, to put her work before the general public as it was to put that of Cézanne a quarter of a century ago ...

Ivy herself made no claim to be an innovator, and was often drily humorous about the more preposterous assertions advanced on her behalf. But at the start of her career she too had struggled, as fiercely as Cézanne and his successors, in the grip of a dead aesthetic orthodoxy. There is no mistaking the reader's sense of relief and liberation on switching from the stifling, sombre, humourless and increasingly frantic convolutions of *Dolores* to the clarity and light, the bold colours and hard outlines of the later novels: "an icy sharpness prevails in the dialogue", wrote Elizabeth Bowen, reviewing *Elders and Betters* in May, 1941. "In fact, to read in these days a page of Compton-Burnett dialogue is to think of the sound of glass being swept up one of these London mornings after a blitz."

Ivy's books sold in large numbers in the second war to a general public which responded for once without reservations to the severe and startling honesty of a writer whose moral economy had, so to speak, always been organised on a war footing. The effect of stiffness and surface distortion no longer seemed a problem in a world where the comforting half truths, clichés and conformist platitudes of convention were temporarily in abeyance. Ivy was after all an almost exact contemporary of Picasso and today, more than a century after her birth, readers may well feel inclined to agree with Elizabeth Bowen, who found complaints about her technical oddity beside the point: "Miss Compton-Burnett, as ever, makes few concessions; she has not, like some of our writers, been scared or moralised into attempting to converge on the 'real' in life. But possibly life has converged on her."

★ ★ ★

"A family is itself", says Hugo Middleton, introducing his own family to a stranger in the opening section of *The Mighty and Their Fall*. "And of course things are hidden in it. They could hardly be exposed." It is a safe bet that circumstances will ensure the systematic exposure of the Middletons' family secrets, which cover a comprehensive field of crime and misdoing from fraud and manslaughter to the more insidious forms of duplicity, greed and emotional blackmail thrown up by the head of the household's blatantly sexual attachment to his twenty-year-old eldest daughter.

The widowed Ninian Middleton has long been accustomed to help himself to attention and affection from the dependants who revolve around him, ranging in age from his eighty-seven-year-old mother to his two youngest children, Hengist and Leah, a hardbitten couple of jokers who are ten and eleven. The price he pays is to find his smallest and most intimate actions laid open to the interested gaze of sharp-tongued and inquisitive onlookers, chief among them the self-deprecating Hugo ("They say there are things worse than honest failure. And I suppose I must be one of them"), a type whose wit, charm and sensitive penetration appealed strongly to Ivy Compton-Burnett in both life and literature. It is Hugo who does his best to ease the shock of a first meeting with the family for Ninian's bewildered future wife:

"He simply said he had a mother and five children."
"Simply!" said Hugo. "And you thought you could have a life that was what it seemed!"

Ninian himself is an exuberant autocrat. He possesses all the qualities Ivy pointed to when people indiscriminately attacked her tyrants: intelligence, honesty, humour, courage, and the grasping, glittering energy that makes him so difficult for the young and inexperienced to resist. There is a powerful fascination about a character who, as Hugo says, combines a Greek god's careless lack of inhibition with the rapacity of the

Biblical patriarch:

"I have never believed in God. I believe in him now. We have known he is a father. And I see that he is yours. There are the anger, jealousy, vaingloriousness, vengefulness, love, compassion, infinite power. The matter is in no doubt."

Second only to Ninian is his formidable parent, Selina Middleton. Tough, shrewd, clear-eyed and unyielding, she surveys the doings of her descendants with "an expression that varied between grim disillusionment and almost unconscious benevolence". Nothing can surprise Selina. She is unshockable, and needs to be to cope with the scarcely less intrepid, obstreperous and unsquashable Hengist and Leah, who are made of considerably sterner stuff than some of their cowed and downtrodden predecessors in earlier novels. These two give and expect no quarter ("'Are you leaving that on your plate, Leah?' said Selina. 'Yes. Only an animal could eat it.' 'And she couldn't leave it anywhere else,' said Hengist".) Selina is what Ivy's friend, the novelist Elizabeth Taylor, called "a perfectly sound agnostic like everybody else", but scepticism does not stop her bringing up her grandchildren to believe in the Almighty, or defending her policy frankly and with spirit:

"They need to accept an All-seeing Eye. Or rather we need them to. No ordinary eye could embrace their purposes. We may as well depute what we can."
"Even to an imaginary overseer," said Ninian . . .
"Is not retribution too far away to count?" said Hugo.
"No doubt," said Selina. But the idea of being watched is discouraging. I found it so."

One of the most striking things about Selina is the respect and affection she inspires. There is something profoundly reassuring about her calm sanity and stoicism, her vigour and tenacity of feeling, above all her adamant refusal to be disconcerted. "I am old. I have seen and heard. I know that things are done", she says at one point, speaking in a voice familiar to Ivy's own friends in later life. "Temptation is too much for us. We are not always unwilling for it to be."

Ivy was nearing her eightieth year when she wrote *The Mighty and Their Fall*, putting herself perhaps more fully and freely into it than any of her earlier novels. There had been previous portraits of herself when young: France Ponsonby in *Daughters and Sons* is an example, and so is Clemence Shelley in *Two Worlds and Their Ways*, but both were conceived with difficulty and born of tensions quite unlike the relaxed and mellow mood that allowed Selina to become in some sense a stand-in for her author. She has the writer's omniscient imagination—"an experience beyond the scope of one life"—and also the writer's essentially dispassionate sympathy: "my presence makes no difference. I am on no one's side. I see with the eyes of all of you. It is as if no one was there."

This is a complacent, if far from flattering self-portrait. Ivy, like Selina, was well acquainted with her strengths and weaknesses, and disposed in the closing stages of her life to accept her own and her friends' shortcomings in something very like Selina's spirit of benevolent disillusionment. Ivy's friends, like Selina's grandchildren, were genuinely fond of her, if sometimes puzzled to account for it. Hengist and Leah are devoted to their grandmother. "They feel your bark is worse than your bite," someone explains in a tribute which Selina, speaking once again in Ivy's voice, takes to be no more than her due: "That is an empty saying. Only bark has a place in life. There is no opportunity to bite. I have wished there was."

Hilary Spurling, London, 1990

CHAPTER I

"Agnes first, Hengist second, Leah third!" said Lavinia Middleton, as her sisters and brother contested the access to the cloakroom in the hall. "And don't be too long. Miss Starkie is waiting for you."

"She told us to stay in the garden."

"Only for half-an-hour. How long have you been?"

"Only three-quarters," said Hengist, as if this was a reasonable difference.

"And we are to have the dining-room luncheon. So we don't have to go upstairs."

"Well, one of you should tell Miss Starkie," said their sister, leaning back on the hall bench.

"I don't want to, because I am the boy," said Hengist. "It is not a real reason."

"No one could want to for any reason," said Leah.

"Miss Starkie may not want to wait for her luncheon," said Agnes.

"She ought not to mind," said Hengist. "She should be thinking of higher things."

"Nothing could be higher than food," said Leah. "Perhaps it is too high for her."

They broke into mirth and continued their talk, a short, sturdy pair of eleven and ten, with broad, sallow faces, dark, deep-set eyes and an almost saturnine aspect. Something about them, when together, suggested the sympathy between them. Agnes was a mild-looking girl of fourteen, with blue eyes, narrower features and a placid but resolute expression.

"What is the jest?" said their elder brother, coming up to his sister on the bench.

"Miss Starkie. Something about her thinking of food."

5

"I used to be surprised that she did. It seemed to reduce her to our level."

"Or to raise her to it," said Leah. "Food is on the heights."

"Well, I feel just about on a line with it at the moment," said Miss Starkie's voice. "So I have come down to pursue it, as no one came up to me. I suppose you are to have your share downstairs to-day."

"We were just going to tell you," said Agnes.

"I have had to take the will for the deed. It is already later than usual."

"Were you assailed by pangs of hunger?" said Hengist.

"Well, by something milder than those. But I did feel Nature's reminder."

"It is kind of Nature to pay attention to her," said Leah to her brother.

"Well, Nature and I are at one at the moment," said Miss Starkie, lightly. "Now I shall be back at the usual time. So I hope your meal will not be delayed."

"We hope so too," said Hengist. "We are high people, almost on the level of food."

"Well, I am even higher, as I am quite on its level."

"Open the door for Miss Starkie, Hengist," said Lavinia. "You can attain to that height."

"Egbert is doing it. It doesn't take more than one person."

Lavinia Middleton was a tall, upright girl of twenty, with large, grey eyes, curling, brown hair, fine bones that showed in both her figure and face, and a look of sober humour. A suggestion of maturity was the result of her being also an autocrat, an intellectual, a widowed father's companion and a grandmother's support. Egbert, two years older and looking of similar age, was a tall, dark youth with an ironic expression and the children's broad face and head in a better form. The bond between the elder pair was as deep as that between the younger. Agnes depended on herself, and therefore more on her elders.

6

Lavinia surveyed the three, as they crossed the hall, with a smile of indulgent understanding. The smile was as light as the feeling behind it. Her depths were not touched here.

"So you are to eat in here to-day," said their grandmother, meeting them in the dining-room with an appraising eye. "Some household trouble of some kind. You can take your places, so as not to harass your father. Hengist, how often have I told you not to keep your hands in your pockets?"

"I have not counted, Grandma," said the latter, too politely to incur rebuke.

"Take them out. You can find a better use for them."

Hengist did so, but appeared not to have the alternative, and Mrs. Middleton kept her eyes on him without change of expression.

"May I sit by you, Grandma?" said Agnes.

Mrs. Middleton drew out a chair with a faint sigh, as though hardly trusting a grandchild to this extent.

"I don't like this room as well as the schoolroom," said Leah, looking round.

"Does it matter to anyone what you like?"

"No, but I can tell them, if I want to."

"It matters to her," said Hengist. "Nothing matters to other people, that is not to do with themselves."

Selina Middleton gave him a look that measured both him and his words. She was a ponderous woman in the eighties, whose type had descended to her grandchildren, with a massive face and head, eyes whose penetration seemed incongruous with their darkness and depth, and an expression that varied between grim disillusionment and almost unconscious benevolence. Her white hair and insistent presence gave an impression of looks, though she had none. She had never wished for them, never having suspected any lack in her endowment.

"It is a change to have luncheon here," said Agnes. "And to have it with Grandma and Father."

"You say things for people to hear them," said Hengist.

7

"It is a reasonable object," said Lavinia.

"I meant for people to hear, and like her for them."

"Well, you certainly avoid her example."

"Talk would be no good, if no one heard it," said Agnes. "And no one likes nothing but silence."

Selina lifted her hand to enjoin this state. She lost little by forbidding speech, as she was accustomed to communicate without it. She signed to Egbert that he was tapping his foot, and that the movement disturbed her.

"Grandma would not hear those sounds, if we talked as usual," whispered Agnes.

Selina intimated that she still heard this one, and her grandson ceased to cause it.

"She tapped her own foot," said Leah.

"I do as I choose," said Selina, barely uttering the words, as if there was no need for them.

"I wish our family resemblance extended so far," said Egbert.

Selina glanced from his face to her own in a glass. The age and the look in the eyes seemed to deny the likeness. Hers suggested an experience beyond the scope of one life, and she had been heard to observe that she had lived several.

"Do you care for this hush, Grandma?" said Lavinia, as if the silence need not include herself. "It seems to defeat its purpose."

"What is the reason of it?" said another voice, as the children's father entered, and laid his hand on his mother's shoulder in observance of a daily custom. "Are you all at a solemn music? Or has silence a music of its own?"

"This one didn't seem to have any," said Hengist.

"I had borne enough," said Selina, as if this was a normal situation.

"I throw no doubt on it," said her son. "Why are they all in here?"

"There are workmen in the schoolroom, Father," said Lavinia. "The ceiling needed repair."

8

"I wonder how they managed to get at that," said Selina, not referring to the workmen.

"It was the hand of time, Grandma. No one else's."

"I liked the cracks on the ceiling," said Hengist. "They were like a map."

"So you favour educational devices," said his father. "I had not realised it."

Ninian Middleton was a tall, almost handsome man of fifty-six, with the family features in another mould, a difference in the same dark eyes, long, supple hands and nervous movements. His voice was high and uncontrolled, in contrast to Selina's deep and steady one, and he seemed to hear his own words and measure their effect.

He sat down at the table and smiled at his children, and Lavinia took the place at his side and put her hand in his, another accepted custom.

He was followed by his adopted brother, a tall, slender man a little younger than himself, with a narrow, uneven face, pale hair and hands and eyes, and an ease of manner and movement that was almost grace. Hugo Middleton, as he was called, had been adopted by Ninian's father in infancy, on the ground that he was the orphan son of a friend, and had grown up under his name and eventually taken it. Rumour and question had long since been rife and died away. Selina had known no more than this, and had accepted what could not be helped. A largeness in her nature had prevented her from visiting her own doubts on the boy, and their relation had grown almost to that of mother and son. He had been left a competence by her husband, and spent his life in the house. Her second or, as it seemed, third son, and the nearest to her heart, lived abroad and was thought of only by herself.

"Is the table the place for toys, Hengist?" she said in her deepest tones. "What is it you have to hide?"

Her grandson showed a pistol, and in proof of his openness fired it towards her.

She started, suffered the reaction, rose and snatched

9

the pistol and flung it into the waste paper basket.

"Why did you do that, Hengist?" said Ninian.

"Grandma doesn't like it to be hidden."

"Take it out of the basket," said Leah. "It is hidden there."

"You will not, while I am over you," said Selina.

"That will be until you die," said Leah. "So the basket can't be cleared until then."

"Do you think that is funny, Leah?"

"I thought it was," said Hengist, smiling.

"I asked Leah what she thought."

"I didn't think it was as funny as it seems to be," said Leah, looking round.

"The pistol will be kept in the schoolroom," said Ninian. "It is here for the last time."

"May we talk now, Grandma?" said Agnes.

"You can ask your father. He is here now to direct you."

"You know what your grandmother wished," said Ninian.

"It is because Agnes knew, that she asked," said Hengist.

"Are you leaving that on your plate, Leah?" said Selina.

"Yes. Only an animal could eat it."

"And she couldn't leave it anywhere else," said Hengist.

"So that is how you see yourselves. As a pair of wits."

"Only other people can see us. And Leah doesn't mind having human food."

"She will have what I give her," said Selina, choosing what would cause no trouble, and seeming not to consider it.

"Grandma's heart is where it ought to be," said Agnes, in an audible undertone.

"You curry favour," said Hengist. "And that means you don't really have it."

"You may reach the same end by a different path," said Ninian.

"I like his path better," said Leah.

"They are all Grandma's little boys and girls," said Selina, with a sudden benevolence that caused no surprise.

"Lavinia and Egbert are not little," said Leah.

"Perhaps they are to Grandma," said Agnes.

"Father thinks Lavinia is equal to himself," said Hengist.

"Age makes no difference in some cases," said his sister.

"It should have in ours," said Ninian. "I know it has made too little. I often feel I am to blame."

"I have never felt it, Father. And no one else is concerned."

"You must finish your luncheon," said Selina. "Miss Starkie will be coming back."

"So she will," said Egbert. "I used to see it as the basis of life. I regret the days when I was under her."

"I wonder what began the being under people," said Leah.

"Examine into your own heart, and you will know," said her father.

"I would rather go to school than learn at home," said Agnes.

"Well, nothing more will be spent on you," said Selina. "You cost enough."

"Only her food and clothes and her share of Miss Starkie," said Hengist.

"Children do not think about such things."

"They think about everything."

"Well, they never talk about them."

"You know they do," said Leah. "You hear them."

"Hengist and Leah," said Selina, in a deep, sudden tone, "you will accept what I say. You will not differ from me or voice thoughts of your own. When I have spoken, I have spoken. And you must know it."

"I envy you," said Hugo. "When I have spoken, I hardly like to know it myself. It always seems so unnecessary."

"I fear I am late, Mrs. Middleton," said Miss Starkie, who had hesitated on the threshold during Selina's speech. "I should say that I know I am. My landlady was behind the time. But I see that you are still at the table."

Miss Starkie returned to her lodgings for her meals, thereby escaping Selina's eye, and allowing the latter some household economies unsuitable for her own. Ninian's income was derived from the estate, and had lessened in the manner of its kind. It seemed to return to its source, taking his energy with it; and his mother kept a hand on the household expense, not suspecting how little it counted in the main stream.

"Well, what is the subject?" said Miss Starkie, ignoring the conclusion of it.

"There have been more than one," said Hengist.

"Well, may I thrust myself in on the last?" said Miss Starkie, speaking as if her words were humorous.

They might have been so in this case, as Hengist and Leah began to laugh.

"What is the jest?" said Miss Starkie, turning her bright, brown eyes from one to another. She was a short, brisk woman of forty-five, with a full, ruddy face, unrelated features, clothes that were never remembered, though they varied with every occasion, and a general aspect almost improbably true to type.

"There is none," said Selina, her voice implying that this was to be the case.

"Were you planning to play some trick on me?" said Miss Starkie, modifying Selina's expression with this light on her experience.

"No, we weren't talking about you," said Leah.

"Then in what way am I involved, that I cannot know the subject?"

"You might not have been so much involved," said Hengist, smiling.

"Miss Starkie is not concerned with your chatter," said Selina. "You need not trouble her with it."

"Oh, I am not curious, Mrs. Middleton," said Miss Starkie, her voice betraying that she had no need to be. "Children's talk means less than nothing, as you say."

"She didn't say it," said Leah. "And it couldn't mean less than that."

"She feels she had better not be curious," said Hengist.

"And why should she feel that?" said Selina. "Tell us the reason."

"She might feel her living was at stake," said Hengist, as if a question should stand its answer.

"Well, that might be a tiresome threat," said Miss Starkie.

"I don't think she is really so unconcerned," whispered Leah.

"Why should she be anything else?" said Selina.

"Well, if Agnes went to school, a governess might cost too much."

"As necessities have a way of doing," said Miss Starkie, lightly.

"And you might teach the others yourself, to save expense."

"Well, there is an idea," said Miss Starkie. "It would be a novel arrangement. I have been successful in my efforts. You have your own ideas and express them."

"It is not my idea," said Leah. "In old books a mother or grandmother do sometimes teach the girls."

"Does teach," said Miss Starkie, smiling at Selina. "So you have reached the stage of reading books and remembering them. That is encouraging for me."

"It is not for me," said Ninian. "I would not have credited such foolishness. It is too kind to put up with it. I hope it does not mean it is familiar."

"Well, I did not feel much pride in them then, Mr. Middleton. It is not their usual level. Egbert and Lavinia know when to be silent. That is a great thing to have learnt."

"You talk as if people learn everything from you," said Hengist.

"Well, everything is a large order, Hengist."

"What other sources of information have you had?" said Ninian.

"A good many things come to people of themselves."

"And those sometimes need correcting," said Miss Starkie, shaking her head.

"Hengist's destiny is school," said Ninian. "He will get his correction there. He will find a change."

"Ah, it will be deflating, Mr. Middleton. Sometimes I think too much so. The balance may be better kept elsewhere. It is only my own view, of course."

"It is mine," said Egbert. "It is the only civilised one."

"And mine," said Hugo "I have never joined the herd."

"Girls do as well as they need at home," said Selina.

"So they will always be here," said Hengist. "It is better to be a girl."

"Oh, *always* is a long word," said Miss Starkie, in an easy tone that covered relief. "As far as we need look forward."

"I wish I could be here too. I would rather learn from a woman."

"Well, I can understand that, Hengist. And I think the view has thought in it."

"It has," said Ninian. "We see the line it takes. I hope he will remember his debt to you."

"People are always taught, when they are young," said Leah.

"Ah, the person who lays the foundation, Mr. Middleton! It is not there that the credit accrues. It is the finishing part that earns it, the part that shows."

"Do you think you are a conceited person?" said Hengist.

"Well, I may have a healthy share of self-esteem. We are none of us the worse for it."

"I think some people might be."

"Why is it healthy?" said Leah.

"Oh, I think you must wait to understand that."

"I hope your patience will meet success," said Ninian. "I have no great hope of it."

"It rests with me to see that it does. We must look into the distance," said Miss Starkie, suggesting the scope of her effort. "It can only come with time. We will not push too far forward. We must not wish our lives away. And school cannot have the fine edge of family life. But we must not complain. It does not claim to have it."

"It is the other side that seems to make the claims," said Selina.

"Well, well, we know our aims, Mrs. Middleton, and see no reason to hide them. And if we sometimes fall short of them, well, we are the better for having them. And now we must start for our walk. Is Lavinia coming with us?"

"No, I am staying indoors. Father is at home to-day."

"Are we to have your escort, Egbert?"

"No, four charges might be too much for you."

Miss Starkie walked after her pupils, upright and conscious after her self-exposure.

"I will be the first to speak," said Hugo, "and will spare the rest of you. Few of us dare to voice aspirations. And I see the reason."

"We can hardly criticise these," said Ninian.

"Or any others," said Lavinia. "Aspirations are always high. I hope something will come of them."

"My children hardly have what I had myself. It is the last thing I wished. But the land does poorly, and giving it my life does not better it. There is little help for my girls or hope for Hengist. I must face the truth and so must they."

"I have taken no harm, Father. I have been able to grow into myself. It has been best both for you and me."

"It could be put in another way. As you grow up, the wrong becomes greater. We should think how to amend it."

15

"I have no tenderness for my age. I have become un-fitted for it. And I can be old or young at will. It is what the house requires of me."

"You should always be young. You have been forced out of your time. In your childhood it was a small thing. It becomes a grave one now."

"We can't retrace our steps. And I have always seen my way. Miss Starkie is outside and will second me."

"Lavinia's way was straight and firm from the first, Mr. Middleton. I can hardly look back without a smile at the sturdy figure forging onwards," said Miss Starkie, right in her mistrust of herself. "Speaking metaphorically, of course."

"I am glad it is not literally," said Hugo. "I could not bear to think of anyone as sturdy, least of all Lavinia. Of course there are people who might be described in that way. But I should not refer to it any more than to any other disability. I should seem to be unconscious of it."

"How much sense do you think you are talking?" said Selina.

"Now that is not fair, Mrs. Middleton," said Miss Starkie. "To sit there in your easy-chair, appearing to be half-asleep—appearing to be absent-minded, and to be alert and critical all the time! We had better set out before we betray ourselves further."

She left the house with her pupils, and Selina moved to the window to observe their progress. Agnes walked in front with Miss Starkie, and Hengist and Leah together behind, indeed arm-in-arm, though this was not their habit. Selina beckoned to her son and returned to her seat. Ninian succeeded her at the window and in a moment leaned out of it.

Something depended from Miss Starkie's skirts, of a nature to unravel when pulled, and her pupils were putting a foot on it in turn, and receding as its length increased.

"Miss Starkie, you have suffered a mischance! Some

part of your dress is disintegrating. The mischief should be arrested."

Miss Starkie turned, paused and stooped, and set off in another direction.

"Oh, a bush will serve me, Mr. Middleton. I can manage in a moment. Why did you not tell me, children?"

"For a reason that is clear," said Hugo. "Some chances do not come again. Sometimes I regret my childhood. But only for light reasons."

"I regret it for deeper ones," said Selina. "Children are always with us. Now one of mine has left me."

"Well, I must go to my work," said Ninian. "I shall soon have Egbert's help. His playtime is nearly over."

"We are too used to the idea of work to realise its meaning," said Hugo. "I had early suspicions of it, and dared to act on them."

"What a comment on life," said Lavinia, "that to be out of work is held to be sad and wrong!"

"Satan lies in wait for idle hands," said Selina.

"But only Satan, Grandma. And he is hardly seen as a model of behaviour."

"My playtime, Father!" said Egbert. "What a description of an Oxford life! And I am sure I am a person who has never played."

"I believe I am too," said Lavinia, "or have come to be."

"It may be true of you both. It comes of the motherless household. It is strange that I have a mother, and you have not."

"I do not fill the place," said Selina. "I have left it empty. I am not a woman who loves her grandchildren as her own. They are further down the scale."

"The two youngest almost too far," said Ninian. "It is Miss Starkie's task to force them up. Few people could undertake it. She seems to be bringing them back. It has begun to rain."

Selina went into the hall, fixed her eyes on her two youngest grandchildren and spoke in deep tones.

"Hengist and Leah, come in where we can see you. And look me in the face. Can you say you did nothing wrong when you were out to-day?"

There was a pause.

"We could," said Hengist. "But it would not be true."

"And that would be doing wrong indoors as well," said Leah.

"Hengist, you thought we did not know. But there was Someone Who knew. Can you tell me Who saw what you did, and saw into your hearts as you did it?" Selina had no religion herself, but feared to let her grandchildren do without it.

"Well, God sees everything. And so in a way he can't see anything. He must pass it over."

"Leah and Hengist, He passes over nothing. What is there in your minds and lives that He does not know?"

"There isn't much in our lives. Even Miss Starkie can't say there is."

"And she sometimes says there is nothing in our minds," said Leah. "So he must have put it into them to do what we did."

"I don't think you needed help," said Ninian.

"But he knows that children are innocent," said Leah, her face grave.

"Well, of course he is one by himself," said Hugo.

"What has Miss Starkie to say?" said Selina, resorting to the human sphere.

"Well, I am surprised and disappointed, Mrs. Middleton. I should be sorry to say I was not. I am glad Agnes did not join."

"I thought something was happening," said the latter. "But it seemed better not to look behind."

"Ah, let us keep our eyes straight in front of us," said Miss Starkie, illustrating the suggestion with her own. "That will be the way to steer our course."

"Miss Starkie is very kind to you," said Ninian. "I hope you know it."

"She has to take us as we are," said Leah.

"Indeed she does not. She will be wise to insist on a difference."

"She might suppress our natural selves," said Hengist. "And there is never gain without loss."

"I think there are cases of it."

"My lessons keep turning up, Mr. Middleton. They will find their setting in time."

"Self-satisfaction is their snare," said Selina, addressing her grandchildren's backs, as they left the room. "That is what they should pluck out and cast from them."

"But it does not offend them," said Lavinia. "The condition is not met. And we all have our share of it."

"I am surprised by mine," said Hugo. "I should not have thought I should have any. I don't know why I have."

"Perhaps this pair are entitled to it," said Selina, turning her eyes on her elder grandchildren.

"They are indeed by themselves," said Ninian. "I fear I bear heavily on them. Lavinia would have had a different life, if her mother had lived."

"Perhaps not a better one. She may not look back and wish it different."

"It is for me to do that. For her and myself and all of us. I live with the might-have-beens."

"Oh, I hope not, Father," said Lavinia. "They should be left where they are, in the receding past."

"They may be a guide for the future. There are lessons in our memories."

"There is usually reproach in them," said Hugo. "It may be the same thing. Is it not time for tea? I did not have very much luncheon. It was Hengist who did."

"There was cold food on the sideboard," said Ninian.

"I saw there was. And I saw it was cold. You are always so right, Ninian."

"You can ring for tea, if you want it," said Selina. "It is almost time."

The bell was answered by the young butler, who glanced

at Selina, turned to the door, and transferred a tray from an unseen hand to the table in one smooth movement.

"Did a spirit bring it?" said Hugo.

"It was Percival, sir," said Ainger, in a tone that deprecated both the name and its bearer. "The new boy, if you have happened to notice. He is a pair of hands."

"Then is he a sort of spirit? That he is so nearly disembodied."

"You should see him at table, sir. You would hardly apply the term."

"Must we call him *Percival*?" said Selina. "What about the name of the last boy?"

"I made the suggestion, ma'am. And the rejoinder was that he was himself. A small point compared to others' convenience!"

"The other name was James," said Selina, considering it by itself.

"That is the case, ma'am. And it could well be the present one."

"Well, arrange it in that way. And if necessary, refer to me."

"I will exert my authority, ma'am," said Ainger, as he left the room.

"Ainger does well in life," said Hugo. "I wonder if he thinks the same of me. I can hardly bear the stamp of success."

"It may be true of us all," said Ninian. "The future does call for help. It is our time to move forward. We must remember the years ahead. There must be change in life. Indeed life itself is change."

"It ends in death," said Lavinia. "There is no need for haste. We go forward only too surely."

"You talk in borrowed words," said her father, smiling.

"And you talk in riddles," said Selina.

"Well, the answer will come in its time."

"Have your father's words a meaning?" said Hugo

to Lavinia. "Is anything coming that will throw us on each other?"

"I don't think there is any fear."

"I thought there might be hope."

CHAPTER II

"Something is on us," said Ainger. "There is something in the air. Well, we shall soon find out."

"I am not one to ferret," said the cook. "As I am not made on that line."

"Well, he who has ears to hear! I am not sorry to have them."

"You need not continue, Ainger. I am not a party to it."

Ainger took his place by the kitchen fire, and Cook stood by him with a severe expression. She was a thin, sallow, middle-aged woman, with odd but definite features, undisguisedly toil-worn hands, and small, grey eyes that seemed to pierce any surface, and generally did so. Ainger was a tall man of twenty-eight, with a fresh, florid face, a broad, boyish nose, and blue eyes that penetrated nothing, which was perhaps why he used his ears. The bond between them did not come from their difference, but from their position above their fellows, which held them to a life apart.

"Well, the truth will come out," said Ainger, turning on his heels. "Not that much seems to come to me."

"Some things are withheld," said Cook, looking unsympathetic towards this bearing. "We need not overestimate ourselves."

"Well, no one saves us the trouble," said Ainger, correcting it as if unconsciously. "And we can make a guess. Perhaps Mr. Hugo is going to be married. Well, he is not too young."

"You need not make comments. And that is not my conjecture."

"And you could not ever be wrong?"

"It might constitute an exception. But I take no credit."

"Well, any change is better than none."

"It depends on the nature. You should weigh your words."

"The master will be in for luncheon. Straws point the way of the wind. It may mean the revelation. I aim to set the table for the whole party."

"For the family," said Cook, looking at him.

"And I shall be on the alert. Either at the table or behind it."

"Ainger, you are in a mood. I pay no regard, as I see no reason."

"Well, we have had no event for a long time."

"And does that indicate that one is imminent?" said Cook, in a severe tone. "Not that I am without an opinion."

"You are afraid to state it, in case it is erroneous."

"I await what comes from the source. It is as yet sealed from our eyes."

This was not to be the case much longer.

Ninian joined his family at the table, but was silent during the meal. At its end he rose, clenched his hands unconsciously, and spoke in a high, even tone, with a forced note of ease.

"I have a word to say. You have been expecting to hear one. I have felt something on my side, as you have on yours. Shadows are cast before. You know what my life has been. It is to be that no longer. You are to welcome someone in the stead of the mother you have lost. I do not say to replace her. That could not be, either for you or for me. But the blank in our life will be disguised, if not filled. And I will not deny that for me it is in a measure to be filled."

The silence was broken by Selina.

"So that is what it is. We might have known. We shall soon feel we did know. So you are what you would naturally be. That is what we should have known. My son, may it all go well with you."

"I knew my mother would wish it. And I want to hear that my children do. When a thing goes without saying we like the better to hear it said."

23

"We can only say it does go without saying, Father," said Egbert.

"He speaks for us all, Father," said Lavinia. "And that does the same."

"Thank you, my dear ones," said Ninian, just turning his eyes on his daughter. "I looked to hear it, and am happier for having heard."

"If you are happy, Father, we have what we want," said Agnes.

"You sound as if you are excited," said Hengist.

"She may be," said Ninian. "And so may you all. It is a great change that is coming."

"I am not excited," said Leah. "We don't know what the difference will be."

"Well, you will soon know," said Selina. "It will not be kept from you."

"Do you wish me well, Hugo?" said Ninian.

"I have no thought over from myself. Does she know about me?"

"Know that you exist?"

"Yes, there is nothing else to be known."

"I have told her about us all."

"A mother-in-law and five stepchildren cannot be helped. But it must seem to her that I could have been avoided."

"Fifty-four years have made their claim," said Ninian.

"To justify my being here? Well, it might take as long. I am fortunate if it takes no longer."

"Will Father still like Lavinia as much?" said Hengist.

"I shall like her better," said Ninian, at once. "I shall see her as the first of my little daughters, instead of the one I have forced out of due time. My reproach will be taken away."

"What will be taken from me, Father?" said Lavinia, in a light tone. "Perhaps not a reproach."

"What has been taken is your childhood. It is I who

have taken it. It is for me to give it back, before it is too late."

"It is too late," said Hengist. "She can't be a child now."

"She can to her father. In a sense she has always been. Another relation has been imposed on the real one. And it is the second that goes deep."

"Perhaps that is why it was harder to see it," said Hugo.

"Lavinia and I will be more equal," said Agnes. "There are only six years between us."

"I have forgotten it," said her father. "I must remember it now."

"You know what you ask of Lavinia, Father?" said Egbert. "We wish you all that is good. We accept many of your words. But we must say one of our own."

"Oh, all's fair in love and war," said Ninian, in a light, almost ruthless manner, admitting a stress on the word, *love*. "She is a person who would know that."

"Would a child know it?" said his daughter.

"I felt you would. I have found I can depend on you. You have wanted me to find it."

"She is to have her wish," said Hugo.

"Will Grandma still live with us?" said Agnes. "Or will she have another house?"

"Perhaps the new wife will not want her," said Hengist.

"Or want you either," said Selina. "Or want any of us. We are not what she wants."

"But a father has to keep his children." said Leah.

"Well, I want all of you," said Ninian. "And she is ready to share you with me. And I will share her with you, if you do not take too much of her."

"Why should we want to share her?" said Leah. "When we haven't seen her, and she doesn't want any of us."

"No, you have not seen her," said Ninian, as if he need say no more.

"Now I am interrupting an occasion?" said Miss

Starkie. "The voices warned me that the schoolroom was deserted. And I had no wish to reign in solitary state."

"It is an occasion indeed," said Ninian. "Or I hope I may say it is. I have been breaking a piece of news to them, the news of my coming marriage. Now that it is broken, I am sure you will congratulate me."

"There is no need to say it, Mr. Middleton. And I would congratulate someone else, if convention allowed it. As it is, I do so in my heart. Well, children, you have had great news. You will find it hard to settle down."

"If you think we can't, I suppose we shan't have to," said Leah. "What difference will it make?"

"None, if I can help it. And I will not countenance much. We know our standard."

"She doesn't want there to be any change," said Leah to Hengist.

"Not for the worse, certainly," said Miss Starkie. "It would be an odd wish. If you can make one for the better, I will be the first to welcome it. "

"Suppose the——the new wife wants to teach us herself?" said Leah.

"Well, I see no reason to suppose it," said Miss Starkie, laughing. "I think you take an optimistic view of yourselves and your requirements."

"It would save expense for herself and Father," said Hengist. "She will be his wife and will share everything."

"Well, I don't think you can expect her to share *you*. It will be my task to keep you from encroaching on her."

"Father said she would share all of us with him," said Leah.

"Oh, in that sense," said Miss Starkie, and dismissed the subject.

"Will she be over Grandma, or will Grandma be over her?" said Hengist.

"What a question to ask! They will not see things in that way."

"She will manage the house, and Grandma will advise her," said Ninian. "So both the ideas are true."

"Will she be glad to have children?" said Leah.

"Stepchildren," said Lavinia.

"Will they make her more important?"

"Well, it would hardly be thought. They will show that her husband has had a life with someone else."

"Do you mean with Mother or with you?" said Hengist.

"I meant with Mother. But it has been with both."

"Well, now it will be with neither," said Ninian, with his ruthless note. "It cannot be with the one, and should not have been with the other. It is a thing that need not be said."

"And so need not have been," said Hugo.

"And people do not think in that way," said Miss Starkie to her pupils.

"How do they think?" said Lavinia. "Is there another way?"

"You must prevent this child from being too mature and cynical, Miss Starkie," said Ninian, with a hand on his daughter's shoulder. "It is my fault that she talks beyond her years, without the knowledge to justify it. It is for you to put it right, as you have put right so much."

"Is it not for you, Ninian?" said Hugo. "It is you who have made the mistake and want it rectified."

"That is my reason for leaving it in better hands than mine."

"Lavinia has learnt so many things easily and well, Mr. Middleton, that I am sure she will learn this. If she has been drawn too soon into the grown-up world, it will do her no harm to realise it. And perhaps she can have a foot in both worlds. That would be a fair compromise. We must try to see the matter through her eyes."

"Well I must go," said Ninian. "I need not say to whom. I am happy in not having to go far. But I shall be happier when we can both stay."

The silence after he had gone was ended by Miss Starkie.

27

"Well, we have had a break in our day. We must go and do better with the rest. I think Lavinia and Egbert will be staying with their grandmother."

"So she knows I should not be alone," said Selina. "And she knows people have a right to what is theirs. What use is wisdom in the wrong place?"

"Is she too good to be a governess?" said Agnes, lingering behind.

"Few people are too good for things. And no one is too good to be left unprovided for."

"You will not be the mistress any longer, Grandma," said Egbert. "I can't keep the thought to myself."

"I have had that change before. I don't know what I shall be. It is for someone else to decide. I daresay she has done so."

"What power a woman can have!" said Lavinia. "And how she can be in the power of another! Father must have known it."

"I wonder if this one can use power," said Egbert.

"Not without misusing it," said Selina. "Few of us can do that. There is little hope that she is one of them. And we see that she will have it."

"What shall I do in the times when I was alone with Father?" said Lavinia, taking refuge in open words.

"What I shall," said her grandmother. "There will be nothing to do."

"Not for me," said Hugo. "I shall spend more time with Lavinia. I don't know if I am grateful to Ninian or vindictive towards him. People can be unsure of their own feelings. It means they have two kinds."

"Grandma, will you leave us?" said Egbert. "We must say the things that are not for you to hear."

Selina nodded and left the room, lifting her shoulders in resignation to her duties, as long as they remained to her.

"So Father is to marry a wife," said Egbert. "It is very masculine of him. I have always appreciated his feminine streak. And now I am afraid it is not there."

28

"People ought not to marry openly," said Hugo. "It is one of those things that should be recognised but veiled."

"It is humbling to accept what is to do you harm," said Lavinia. "It means you put others before yourself, and naturally that is despised. It is odd that it is held to be esteemed."

"I was grateful to you and Miss Starkie, Uncle," said Egbert. "Father can't shut his eyes to all human claims."

"He said all was fair in love and war. I have always thought it an immoral saying."

"It means the opposite of what it says. But why say all is unfair in love and war? We all know it. Anyhow Father does."

"He feels I have failed him," said Lavinia. "And knows it would be worse for him, if I had not."

"He is too sunk in his own life to remember anything," said Egbert.

"And we are to find that comforting? Suppose we followed his example!"

"This will pursue us to the end. In old age we shall remember being cast from our place."

"In our youth we shall suffer it. And it may lead to things we can foresee."

"I did not dare to ask Father what she was like," said Egbert.

"I purposely did not ask him. I did not want to show interest in her. And so showed how much I had."

"I hope I shall never have the feelings of a normal man," said Hugo. "I am sure he is more normal than anyone else."

"May I clear the table now, sir?" said Ainger, at the door, looking past Lavinia, as though to spare her.

"Yes, clear it, of course. Other people will be coming in."

"So the news has transpired, sir," said Ainger, as he

29

pursued the task. "Changes come and carry us with them."

"That sounds more comfortable than it is."

"This one was a surprise, sir? Those who are nearest! They may be too close to see."

"That might be fortunate for them, if the closeness retained its virtue. But it loses it at the critical moment. Do you mean you were prepared?"

"Well, the wind blows, sir. And we know what is said."

"I suppose it is always doing that," said Lavinia. "I wonder more does not happen."

"Well, an amount does, miss. Might I perhaps step to the door? The cloth for the crumbs escaped my memory."

"Oh, come in, Cook. So you were not surprised by the news?"

"Well, it was a matter of intuition, miss. And that has never been my weak side."

"It seems it was ours, and that of the whole family."

"Well, what is under our eyes, miss. And in your case experience was wanting."

"Well, we have it now. And it is held to be an advantage. Though it can seem an odd view."

"You put a face on it, miss," said Cook, with a sympathy blunter than Ainger's. "It is what is due. Some must not betray themselves."

"How do you feel about having a new mistress?" said Egbert.

"It is a premature enquiry, sir. We have not dwelt on the matter. We have our occupations."

"Surely this is one of them," said Lavinia.

"Well, miss, it remains uncertain. We can only wait."

"But all things come when we do that. It will do no good."

"The master has his rights, miss. It has to be said."

"It seemed it did have to. We all said it. I think he did so the most."

"We are all held to have them," said Ainger. "But I have asked myself what they are in my case."

"Then you can answer yourself, Ainger," said Cook. "You do not happen to be the subject."

"Do you think about yours, Cook?" said Hugo. "It is a thing I have not had to do, as I am without them."

"It is not a point to dwell on, sir. I have my place."

"And I have mine," said Ainger. "And it seems I shall always have it."

"If you fill it, Ainger, and with your might," said Cook. "The question has another side."

"Well, fate can strike any of our party at any time," said Ainger, whose speech gained freedom in the absence of Selina and Ninian.

"And whom do you include in the term? You are not coupled with those otherwise placed."

"Destiny is over all of us, high or low."

"And is it for one of the last to express the matter?"

"The candlesticks tarnish, miss," said Ainger, polishing one as a pretext for lingering. "And things will have to be in shape. You have not seen the lady, I suppose?"

"Did you not use your ears at luncheon?" said Egbert.

"Well, his place was there, sir," said Cook, in a condoning manner.

"Yes. Where else was he to use them?"

"How I used mine!" said Hugo. "I could not have borne to be anywhere else."

"Only some of us should have ears," said Ainger, shaking out his leather.

"Is the candlestick tarnishing already?" said Egbert.

"You need not touch on distinctions, Ainger," said Cook. "There are states of life and we are called."

"   'When Adam delved and Eve span,
        Who was then the gentleman?' "
murmured Ainger, with a hint of revolving on his heels.

"And did you happen to be on the spot, then?"

31

"No, I have never heard there was a third. And anyhow it was not your humble servant."

"Ainger, if it is a subject for lightness, it is time to withdraw. And do you think no one is present?"

"I regret the withdrawal," said Egbert. "I needed comfort and I have had it."

"So have I," said Lavinia. "People in trouble are easily grateful. It confirms that we are in it."

"What are you in?" said Selina, entering with her son.

"In a new position," said Egbert.

"You make too much of it," said Ninian. "Gossiping in here together! Why did you not go with the others?"

"You know we often stay behind," said Lavinia. "Or you did know until to-day."

"There is safety in numbers," said Egbert. "Do we need the protection of the herd?"

"Your place is with it. Do you see yourselves as people apart?"

"As apart from the children. That is how we are seen. It is what we are."

"You need not magnify the gulf. You can prove the parable of the faggot, if you hold together. But you must not make my wife and me afraid of you. Not that she is afraid of much."

"Describe her to us, Father," said Lavinia.

"Oh, you will see her for yourselves. There is no need to hurry forward. She has not asked for a description of all of you."

"It would have been rash," said Hugo. "Perhaps something warned her."

"What are we to call her, Father?"

"Oh, it will be for her to say. I don't know how she will see you. It may depend on yourselves."

"What would you like yourself, Ninian?" said his mother. "You must have thought of it."

"If you will believe me, I had not. There will be time

to consider it. She will have enough of names. I have not deluged her with them."

"You were wise," said Egbert. "She has not Miss Starkie's experience."

"She will feel her own," said Ninian, "if she is to be subjected to this."

"How old is she, my son?" said Selina. "It is odd that I have not asked."

"None of you can be accused of that kind of oddness. She is my age or a little older."

"So there will be no children. Well, you will feel there are enough."

"Yes, there is a full quiver. We do not need to add to it. Our life will be with each other."

"She might like a child of her own," said Egbert.

"What do you know about *her*?" said Ninian.

"Nothing. And it seems we are not to know more."

"You will know in time, as I have said. You hardly seemed so anxious for what was before you."

"That does not mean we should have no idea what it is."

"You will all be at your best with her?" said Ninian, in another tone. "I feel I keep having glimpses of another side."

"Few people can give a shock, without meeting those," said Selina.

"Well, I am not one of them. And there is a risk that it may be remembered."

"Well, do not forget that other people have memories."

"How did you meet her, Father?" said Lavinia. "We can hardly speak of her without asking questions. And there is no one else in your thoughts."

"Not long ago. Not far from here. And quite by chance."

"And you were meant for each other?" said Selina. "So it might have been arranged before. Your mother would have thought of it."

"So it is chance that leads us to retrace our steps,"

said Egbert. "We speak of it too lightly. Nothing seems to achieve so much."

"You show me you have never taken the steps," said Ninian. "You make me wish for someone who has done so. When you and your sister were with me, you did not think of me as having no one but you. You did your best; you could not have done better; I am grateful to you. How could you know that in such a case it is the elder who suffers, that whatever you gave to me, I gave more to you? I ask for no change in yourselves, only that you will be what you have been. It is the change in you that disturbs me."

"There is other change, my son," said Selina. "You cannot expect them not to see it."

"Of course there is change. I feel it in myself. I am doing what I am, to make it. It is time it came. I shall no longer live as the father and guide of other people. I shall live as myself, with someone who can return what I give. You find the change unwelcome? It is not to me. Have you really thought it is? In other words what are you to me?"

"Your mother, my son. It is what I shall always be. And if your wife does this for you, I will be her mother too. And a wary, wise old mother, if that is best for you. It will be what is best for me."

"Some things are best for us all," said Ninian, going to the door. "There is no good in putting our faculties to a doubtful use. I think we all see it."

"So Father has thrown away the past," said Lavinia. "What will he get from the future? We never recover what we have lost. He will not and I shall not."

"They say there is never loss without gain," said Hugo. "I have wondered if it is true. Now I am to lose Ninian, I shall find out. And I think it is."

CHAPTER III

"WELL, HERE IS my family," said Ninian. "The family that will be yours. I will only present my mother. You will distinguish the rest by degrees. This is enough for the moment."

"What are we to call her?" said Hengist, in a low tone.

"Stepmother," said Leah, with her face grave.

"Oh, I hardly think that will do," said Miss Starkie. "And she is not that as yet."

"We shall have to be told something," said Hengist. "Or we must just say *her* and *she*."

"Well, I hope you will not do that. You have been taught better."

"It need not be settled at the moment," said Ninian. "It is hardly an urgent question."

"I had not thought of it," said his future wife. "And it does not matter."

"We could say *Mother*, if she would like it," said Agnes, gently.

"Oh, she does not want to adopt the tribe," said her father. "That is asking too much."

"Agnes didn't ask it," said Hengist. "What she said was different."

"Perhaps my Christian name would do. I can't think of anything better."

"It would be almost worse for children to say, than *she* and *her*," said Leah.

"Well, I know what you mean," said Miss Starkie. "And I can understand the feeling. But it is not for you to decide."

"Luncheon is ready, ma'am," said Ainger at the door.

"Why did he say it to Grandma and not to *her*?" said Hengist.

"Grandma is the mistress of the house," said Ninian. "The change has not come yet. And say *Mrs. Chilton* for the time."

"Mrs.?" said Leah, looking up. "Then has she a husband?"

"No, she is a widow. And you had better know she has no children. She may be congratulating herself on it."

"Now you know everything," said Miss Starkie. "So you need not ask anything more."

"It is not wrong to ask questions," said Leah.

"It can seem the most unsympathetic of failings," said her father.

"Why doesn't she sit at the end of the table, if she is going to be Father's wife? Isn't she equal to him?"

"She isn't until she is married," said Hengist. "Then she will be a little better, because she is a woman."

"Now I don't know what to say," said Miss Starkie.

"Neither do they," said the new-comer, half-smiling. "That is the trouble."

"And one that must be surmounted, Mrs. Chilton."

"So she has said it," said Leah.

Teresa Chilton was an arresting-looking woman of hardly middle height, with a clear, pale skin, dark hair wound about a full-shaped head, features at once ill-drawn and delicate, and eyes of a brown that was almost gold. Her expression was aloof and absent, and she appeared to notice less than she did. Her voice was low and rapid, with little rise and fall.

"Is Lavinia like her mother?" she said to Ninian, as she looked round. "Several of them are so like you."

"Yes, there is a great likeness, greater now she has grown up. Not that she has done so. She is two years younger than Egbert. She has done much for me, and I am grateful to her. But I am glad to lift the burden now. Agnes is the child we can't account for."

"I am the only one with really blue eyes," said Agnes, turning them on Teresa.

36

The latter kept hers on Ninian.

"You can't undo what is past. It is the one thing in a safe place."

"It can be left behind. That must happen with many things."

"Will *she* and Lavinia be equal?" said Hengist. "Or will one be above the other?"

"What a question!" said Miss Starkie. "It does not deserve an answer."

"It had better have one," said Ninian. "*She* will be my wife, and Lavinia the eldest of my girls. There is an end of it."

"Mr. Middleton, may I make a suggestion? Would *Mater* be a good form of address? It is the Latin word for *Mother*, and would be a compromise between the actual word and familiarity. Of course it is only my own idea. But we can never suggest better ideas than our own."

"Well, no one else can offer one at all," said Ninian, seeing Teresa's indifference. "We must accept it and be grateful."

"Well, it is my habit to put my ideas at the general disposal. There is little to be said for keeping them to oneself. There is the chance of their being of help."

"Everyone knows that *Mater* is the Latin word for *Mother*," said Leah.

"Well, I am glad you do. It would not be to my credit, if you did not. It was natural to mention it in this connection."

"They are not usually with us," said Ninian, in reassurance to Teresa. "Their presence is in honour of yours. I don't know if you recognise the tribute."

"Lavinia is with you in the evenings, Father," said Agnes.

"Well, she knows what I shall want of her now. And I trust her, as I always have."

"May I give you some more wine?" said Egbert to Teresa, to cover the moment.

37

"Now add the two words, Egbert," said Miss Starkie. "Set the example. We depend on you."

"What are we making a matter of?" said Ninian. "A word is no more than it is."

"We have come upon an enigmatic example, Mr. Middleton."

"Is Father's marrying supposed to be a good thing for us?" said Hengist.

"It will be," said Miss Starkie. "It will not be a matter of supposing."

"I don't see how it can be much good," said Leah.

"They are children," said Ninian to Teresa. "I don't know if you are familiar with the race."

"She must have been a child herself," said Hengist.

"Now what should it be?" said Miss Starkie.

"Say it again, as you should," said Ninian.

"She must have—Mrs. Chilton must have been a child herself."

"They feel the name takes them out of their world," said Teresa.

"Do you know, I think they do, Mrs. Chilton? It is a step for them to address an adult on equal terms. It is not so long since children said *sir* and *ma'am*. And I think it was a good custom."

"Then used children to be the same as servants?" said Leah.

"They were all supposed to show respect to those above them."

"I don't much care after all to be called *Mater*," said Teresa. "I don't see any difference between the word and *Mother*. They have the same meaning. I am not their mother, and cannot be. That seems to answer the question."

"Of course I meant the suggestion to depend on your wishes, Mrs. Chilton. If it does not meet them, it is as if it had not been made."

"Well, make another, Miss Starkie," said Lavinia. "We are still in doubt."

"I hardly think there is another. It is either equality or the maternal suggestion. Those are the alternatives."

"Some families would say *Mrs. Middleton*," said Agnes. "I mean after they were married."

"This family will not," said her father.

"I quite agree with you, Mr. Middleton," said Miss Starkie. "It has not a suitable touch. I should not care for it."

"I don't mind if they use my Christian name," said Teresa.

"We should feel honoured to do so," said Egbert.

"I shall not say anything," said Hengist. "And neither will Leah."

"Well, Lavinia and Egbert can say *Teresa*, and the rest of you nothing," said Ninian. "That will serve for the time."

"May I say *Teresa*, Father?" said Agnes.

"Well, if you have permission,"

"Yes, she may," said Teresa, hardly uttering the words.

"Well, we are back at the starting-point," said Miss Starkie, lightly. "It is like a race run in a circle."

"Well, it is run," said Ninian. "And I suppose it had to be."

"And there is a victory, Mr. Middleton. I do not dispute it. But it seems rather an empty one."

"Because we are to say nothing?" said Leah. "That seems to make it empty. But the others are to say something."

"It is all rather much for you, Leah?" said Miss Starkie, smiling. "Well, we will leave it for the time."

"Is she older than he is?" said Hengist. "I mean, is she older than Father?"

"So you see a name has its uses," said Miss Starkie. "We find it when we do without one."

"But she knew you meant *her*, when you said *she*," said Leah to her brother.

39

"Do you know if she is older?" said Hengist to Miss Starkie.

"No, it is nothing to do with me."

"But that is when people want to know things the most."

"Oh, I hope not, Hengist. What a view to take! I am glad it is not mine."

"I am a little older than your father," said Teresa, turning her eyes from a portrait to Lavinia's face.

"Yes, there is the real likeness," said Selina. "It is a portrait of her mother."

"I thought it was of herself at first. But of course it is not young enough."

"It is a greater likeness than has ever been known," said Agnes. "It must be nice to be like someone like that."

"Poor *like*!" said Miss Starkie. "You are giving it a great deal to do."

"That may be why Father was fond of Lavinia," said Hengist. "Anyone so like someone else could almost do instead of her."

"Not in this case," said Ninian. "And not in any real one. No one can take the place of anyone else."

"Lavinia did take this one," said Leah. "But she has to go back from it now."

"Why, what an odd phrase!" said Miss Starkie.

"It meant what she meant it to mean," said Hengist.

"Dear, dear, how you overwork your words! I feel quite sorry for them."

"I have never seen Lavinia cry before," said Leah, in a sudden awed tone.

"You need not see it now," said Hengist, roughly.

"No, do not notice it," said Miss Starkie, speaking very low. "You know how you feel when you cry."

"I sometimes do it to make people notice me."

"That is because you are young," said Hengist.

"I will cry with Lavinia," said Hugo. "And then

40

people will have to notice us. And I hope they will be upset."

"Egbert, have you taken a vow of silence?" said Ninian.

"It would be better if I had, Father. It would be an excuse."

"It is not such a difficult occasion."

"I think it is," said Teresa, without a smile. "It has to be; and not only for them."

"You are finding it so? You need not be alarmed. They are no worse than they seem."

"I am not alarmed," said Teresa, as if she might be other things.

"Would you like to have some children?" said Leah, looking at her. "I mean some of your own?"

"She could hardly want any more of mine," said Ninian.

"We can't help being here," said Hengist.

"Now who suggested that you could speak?" said Miss Starkie. "You should think before you speak."

"I don't feel I am here," said Hugo. "And I hope nobody knows I am."

"I should not be," said Egbert, "if it were not for Lavinia. I get my reality from her, and always shall."

"There, Lavinia!" said Miss Starkie. "There is a foundation for your future."

"And what is that?" said Ninian.

"Her brother's dependence on her, Mr. Middleton. It is a rare and real thing," said Miss Starkie, looking aside as she relinquished restraint.

"They must release each other in time for their lives to grow."

"Releasing is a very wicked thing," murmured Egbert.

"What did you say?" said Ninian.

"I said it to Lavinia, Father."

"Now will you say it to me?"

"I said that releasing was—might be a wicked thing."

"Oh!" said Ninian, in light dismissal of this. "The same old puzzle for you! That I do not belong to anyone, body and soul."

"Does he not?" said Lavinia to her brother.

Ninian looked sharply at her, but checked his words.

"How much will you belong to me?" said Teresa. "With all this force drawing you away."

"As much as it is right to belong to anyone. As much as I shall ask you to belong to me. But as much as that for our lives."

"There is the difference," said Lavinia. "It cannot come to an end. No, I shall not repeat it, Father. We must be allowed to speak to each other. We have not been struck dumb."

"I think people should talk to me," said Hugo. "It is their duty to include me in the occasion. Suppose I felt I was an alien after all!"

"I will talk to you," said Teresa. "And ask you about this family, and all that is hidden in it. I feel I have never met one before."

"You have not met this one. A family is itself. And of course things are hidden in it. They could hardly be exposed. You will be wise not to know about them. Think of Miss Starkie, spending her life trying to keep them hidden."

"I should not aim at her level. But I need some help on my own."

"No, you would try to use it. You must live your life with Ninian, and forget everything besides. It is the best chance for you and him."

"But not a very good one. He will not forget everything but me. There will be too many reminders. I should like to have a life that was what it seemed. But I see no hope of it."

"It is a pity you did not know Ninian's family, as you came to know him."

"Yes. He simply said he was a widower with a mother and five children."

"Simply!" said Hugo. "And you thought you could have a life that was what it seemed! Not that what it seems is not enough. Cannot you be content with it?"

"Content to live on the surface, with all this simmering underneath?"

"Why not be thankful that that is where it is?"

"I should think your life is very much what it seems."

"I am afraid it is. I am so ashamed that I show it. I should not dare to share it with anyone, in case she assumed that things were hidden in it, and asked me what they were."

"It would be good to hear there was none."

"But a shared life might bring them. And I should not know how to deal with them. I have only looked on."

"What are you doing now?" said Ninian. "Do you feel it is your duty to converse with the guest, in accordance with some social code? It is not a formal occasion."

"We are talking deeply. And deep things never come to an end. And almost everything seems to be deep."

"You must not tire Teresa. She is not used to a large family."

"That is what I felt. I thought I should be a rest for her."

"It hardly sounds as if you were."

"He gave me calming advice," said Teresa. "I am to live on the surface and forget what is beneath. Your past with your wife and daughter would be thrust down and forgotten."

"My daughter! Is that never to be laid to rest? Things could not have gone on much longer. Her life must develop apart from mine."

"She may feel it is happening in the opposite way."

"So it is. But it will happen with her in the end. It is her time to be free. It is strange that people do not see it. And it is stranger that you should belong to them. It is something I did not look for."

43

"It is for yourself that you are making the change, my son," said Selina, in a low tone. "If it were not, you would not be wise to make it. As it is, you are."

"How few people would realise that!" said Hugo. "It is pleasant to hear it stated."

"Then in what way am I a culprit? That is how you all see me."

"In your way of doing it, Father," said Egbert, also speaking low. "You could have chosen a better one."

"Then I should not have done it," said Ninian, drily. "I see I took the only one."

"I wish I was not the cause of all this," said Teresa.

"It had to come," said Ninian. "We see it was the time. I will not have it come again."

"You can feel you are a martyr, Mrs. Chilton," said Hugo. "So you should be experiencing ecstasy."

"A martyr also has honour. I have neither the one thing nor the other. But I almost feel it is what I am. And it seems that the same might be said of someone else."

"Then do not say it," said Ninian. "That is a reason why you should not. Do you think it is the way to serve her? You are surely too wise."

"It may serve her in the end."

"Why do you say so?"

"It was what came into my mind. Well, she has her brother. Perhaps the others need more pity."

"No, they give it," said Hugo. "And it does no harm, when it has enough contempt in it. And their pity has."

"Oh, I have not a brood of little martyrs," said Ninian to Teresa. "I don't know why you think so."

"It might be a definition of a young family. Childhood can be a troubled time."

"The fashion has changed. It used to be the happiest of our lives. Perhaps the truth lies in between."

"It may lie anywhere. And where it is, it often stays."

"Does wisdom lie here?" said Selina, smiling at Ninian. "The problems of your household may be safe in these hands."

"They will not be in them. They are nothing to do with her. She is to be my wife, not the mother of children who are not hers, and the rectifier of mistakes she has not made. That would be a wrong demand. And it seems I have done enough wrong. It is each other we want, not what we can claim from each other. That must be clear."

"Well, it is, my son," said Selina.

"Do all men have two wives?" said Leah's voice. "I mean before they die."

"No, of course not," said Miss Starkie. "But when they lose the first wife, they sometimes have a second."

"But they would always like the first one best?"

"No, it would depend on many things."

"The first would be the real choice," said Hengist.

"I would never be a second," said Leah. "I wonder she agreed to it."

"I wonder she did," said Ninian. "I am grateful to her. And so should you be, if you think of my happiness."

"We haven't ever thought of it," said Hengist. "We didn't know you weren't happy. And we didn't know she was coming."

"Well, you know she is here now."

"Yes, we can see her."

"And she is good to look at, isn't she?"

"Yes, but so is she," said Hengist, looking at his mother's portrait. "I think she is better. I don't think *she* can ever have been quite so good. Even if she was like her. And they are not."

"Dear, dear, I find the pronouns too much," said Miss Starkie. "I wish we could dispense with them."

"No. I have never been quite so good," said Teresa.

"It is a pity she can't hear her," said Leah. "She might be pleased."

"Now should not little people be seen and not heard?"

45

said Miss Starkie, seeing no other solution. "I find myself favouring the old ideas."

"They needn't listen to us," said Hengist. "I don't think *she* does. She is only looking at Lavinia and her."

"Cannot they say *Mamma* or *Mother* of their own mother?" said Teresa. "It would be of some help."

"They do not remember her," said Ninian, "and so do not speak of her. It makes them uncertain how to do it."

"Now I am sure that they—your father and Mrs. Chilton have had enough of you," said Miss Starkie. "It has been kind to be patient with you for so long."

"Your patience has to hold out," said Teresa.

"If it did not, I could not be an educationist, Mrs. Chilton."

"I did not know such people were distinguished by patience," said Ninian. "It was not my experience."

"She meant she could not be a governess," said Hengist to Leah.

"I meant what I said, Hengist. That is what a governess should be."

"Do other people think she is that?" said Leah.

"Come, speak clearly," said Miss Starkie.

"She wouldn't have liked it said so that they could hear," said Hengist.

"And *she* mightn't like us to say it about her, as she seems to like her."

"Come, open the door, Hengist," said Miss Starkie, indifferent to anything but exit. "And wait for your sister and me. You know how to behave."

"I have not met a governess before," said Teresa. "Are they always built on this scale?"

"There is scope for her qualities," said Egbert. "We have made our own demand on them."

"Less than is made now," said Lavinia. "Unless we idealise our earlier selves."

"Memory softens the truth," said Ninian. "But no demand would be denied."

46

"Lavinia was beyond Miss Starkie," said Egbert. "She read by herself, when she was with her."

"Pronouns worthy of our two youngest," said his father.

"You are gaining knowledge," said Hugo to Teresa. "And though I have always lived here, so am I."

"We want more of everything, the more we have. I am impelled to an inquisitive question."

"Well, what other sort of question is there?"

"Is Miss Starkie's work worth while? I don't mean in itself. I mean, can she ask enough return?"

"Of course you mean that. I don't think she asks anything. There are subjects she would not broach. I don't know how much she has, though of course I should like to. It might be too little to be revealed. But Ninian will have no secrets from you. I daresay it would have to be a secret from everyone else."

"I will betray it to you one day," said Teresa.

"Betray what to him?" said Ninian.

"Something you will tell me, that you have not told him."

"Well, there may be things of that kind."

"There must be in a marriage. No doubt you found it in yours. It is a pity the children can't remember their mother."

"It may be better than remembering and missing her."

"It is better," said Lavinia. "Egbert and I know it."

"Yours can only be an early memory. No doubt you have added to it."

"We have our picture of her. It may not be the true one, but it is our own."

"What will Egbert do in the end?" said Teresa.

"He will support me here. He must learn to fill my place. In time it will be his."

"I shall also be here," said Lavinia, looking at Teresa. "There is nothing else for me. Or for you."

"Do not answer things that are not said," said Ninian.

"The question was there, Father. And there was only one answer."

"Lavinia, are you doing your best for me?"

"What are you doing for me? Can I feel this is your best? What have you said to me, and of me? And how have you said it?"

"What I have said is true. It should have been said before."

"But it was not. It has been said too late. You should have known when to be silent."

"Lavinia, I will not suffer this again."

"There is no need. You will remember it."

"It is true that I shall not forget."

"Then it is over," said Selina. "It may have had to come. But there can be no cause for it again."

"Egbert, you will have a care for your sister?" said Ninian, in a tone of genuine appeal. "You see how I am placed."

"Egbert does not need such a word, Father. Our lives are bound together. But there are some things I have tried to spare him. I have been taken further than he has. I have been used to a man."

"You force me to say it. I have not been used to a woman. I am glad to be with one now."

"Nothing should have forced you to say that, Father," said Egbert.

"Should not they leave us?" said Teresa. "They have their life with each other. I have not brought one with me."

"You hear?" said Ninian to his children. "We have heard you."

"I will go in my own time," said Selina. "You cannot dismiss your mother. And my presence makes no difference. I am on no one's side. I see with the eyes of all of you. It is as if no one was here."

"It is not to me," said Ninian. "And so it is not to Teresa. But if you would like to follow the others, I will take you to them. They will be the better."

The two went out of the room, and Hugo turned to Teresa.

"I am forgotten. But of course I should not like them to waste their thought on me."

"You feel that a waste?" said Teresa, raising her eyes. "How unlike you are to your brother!"

"He is not my brother by blood. I was adopted by his father, and brought up with the name. And I have remained in the family. I have no other."

"Ninian has a great affection for you."

"Yes, he has been more than a brother to me."

"And Mrs. Middleton?"

"She has been more than a mother. But I used to wish they were not any more. They would not have been so afraid of being any less."

"And how about the father?"

"He was a little less than a father to me. He left me only just enough for my support. He could not take more from the family. I wish they had all been average."

"Do you feel I am harming Lavinia?"

"I daresay not in the end. She has been more than a daughter to Ninian. And, as I say, that is not best."

"You have been a great help in his life."

"Yes, I have not been more than a brother to him. I have tried to be an ordinary one. But I am hardly bad enough for that."

"Are you very fond of Lavinia?"

"Yes, more than of anyone. I wish I was young and better off. A competence is known to be a curse.

"If it was not known, would you have guessed it? It is surely a step on the way. I understand your feeling for her. I think I could come to share it. She can't want me at the moment. But perhaps she will."

"Remember she is mine," said Hugo. "I would not be more than an uncle to her. And I was not an ordinary one. So there was nothing I could be. But she is mine."

"You have more to give than Ninian has."

"Well, I have had less. I am not so used to taking. But

49

I will not be more than a brother-in-law to you. You need not fear."

"I should be glad for you to be more."

"More than what?" said Ninian, returning to the room. "What a deal you have to say! You might be long-lost friends."

"We are new-found ones," said Hugo. "And brothers should share everything."

"Well, I hope, Teresa," said Ninian, on a mock-serious note, "that our combined influence may do something for Hugo. There are signs of good in him.—And there are signs in my son and daughter, though you have not discerned them."

The two last had gone to the library to be alone, while Selina went up to the children.

"So you have said it," said Egbert. "Well, silence would have been no good. It would always have been unsaid."

"It will never be so now. I can never unsay it. Father will remember. It will always be between us."

"Not as you think. Things go less deep with him."

"We like to feel that about people. But I don't know why. It is a thing that does us little good."

"He is thinking of his own life. And that he has not had what he now thinks he should have had."

"And does he think of no other life, when he is so given to thought?"

"He believes he has done his best. I think he feels it is a poor one. And he is right that it should have been better."

"What is Teresa's feeling for him? She does not show herself. There seems to be a calm surface over unspoken things. But whatever she is or feels, what has this house to give her? It is filled with another woman's family. And her husband must always be their father. Even though she has had one life herself, I wonder she could face this one."

"I wondered too," said Ninian's voice. "She is facing it for my sake. And finding so much could be done for me, I may have asked more of other people than it was in them to give. Do what you can; you cannot go beyond yourselves."

"Neither can anyone," said Egbert. "Even she will want her own return."

"And she will have it," said Ninian, with a flash of his eyes. "All will be done to make this house a home to her, and her own home. It is hers before it is yours or mine. I did not come to say that. It goes without saying. But it is better said."

"What did you come to say, Father?" said Lavinia.

"That you and Egbert can go your way apart from us. You can make the change as great or little as you please. I shall depend on your thoughts for the children, as I always have. It is true that I forgot you were a child yourself, and that it was late to remember it. But neither can be helped now. And I doubt if either could have been helped."

"Well, neither was helped, Father. And both have served your ends."

"Lavinia, you have become a stranger to me."

"I might say the same to you. I do say it. And, as you might put it, it is better said."

"Well, no more will be said," said Ninian, and left the room.

"Well, there are things that have to be," said Egbert.

"And that is a pity. The worst seem to be included in them."

"Are we spoiling Father's happiness?"

"No, our happiness belongs to ourselves. Our own things are safe with us. That may be why it is little liked by other people."

"Teresa hardly seems a happy person."

"Perhaps it helped Father to fall in love with her. Though I see there might be other reasons."

Ninian's exit led to the entrance of Ainger, bearing something carefully in his hands, and followed by the boy in mechanical submission.

51

"The change will be great, miss," he said, depositing what he held, and standing with considering eyes on it.

"It will to us. There will be less difference for you."

"A new mistress in the house, miss! It hardly precludes difference," said Ainger, taking something from his attendant's hand without acknowledgement.

"Do the under servants feel the same as you do?" said Egbert.

"Well, the same is hardly the word between us, sir. As your term indicates."

"What counts is the master's happiness. To him and all of us."

"Yes, sir, in a high sense," said Ainger, as if this must put a limit to the feeling.

"Nothing betrayed, Cook," he said in the hall, putting his arm about her less in romantic feeling than in the assumption of its unlikelihood. "Nothing given away. The truth might be too precious to part with."

"It is the convention among them. They cannot be beneath themselves."

"What is the use of mouths that are kept shut?"

"It is a point you are blind to. You might take a lesson."

"It is little good to take lessons, when you don't take anything else."

"You should abandon that line. All things are not material. Higher ones are the same for all."

"I doubt if everyone is so sure of it."

"Your doubts do not bear on matters. It is certainties to which I allude."

CHAPTER IV

"Well, it is all at an end," said Ninian, standing at the table with a letter in his hand. "Nothing remains of it. Nothing will come of it. The reason is that nothing was in it. It is as if it had not been. As the memory goes, everything will go with it. Nothing will be left. There has been nothing."

He made as if to tear the letter, but checked himself, and stood, tossing it from hand to hand.

"Do you mean you are not going to be married?" said Egbert.

"You have followed me. Would you have meant anything else? Teresa means it, and we must mean it with her. Well, I never really thought it would come to pass."

"Well, I did at first," said Hugo. "And so did we all. So you were the wise one."

"At first?" said Selina, looking at him.

"In the beginning," said Hugo, turning from her to Ninian. "Are reasons given for the change?"

"My large family. My living past. I could not pretend it was dead. My giving only what was left. Her desire for a man who was untrammelled and had a lighter touch on life."

"There almost sounds a message there," said Selina.

"No, your ear is too sharp," said Lavinia. "She said simply what she had to say."

"Well, it made a break for me," said Ninian. "And I admit I found it welcome. The time seemed to have come. But I can leave it behind. I have done so."

"You have many to help you," said Selina. "I wonder if she can say the same."

"One piece of help I will ask. That one of you will tell

the children. I don't need to be present at the scene. I can imagine it."

"I will tell them," said his mother, deepening her tones. "And let no one forestall me. It is a thing to be done by one person, and one alone."

"And that person you."

"That person me, my boy."

"You are silent, Lavinia," said Ninian. "You don't know what to say. And I hardly know myself, though it is for me to say it. If we go back to our old life—and that is what it must seem—I will not expect the same of you. I shall not be the same. I should hardly wish to be. But we should not have lost everything. Something of the past should remain."

"I shall not be different, Father. Any difference will be in you. It is from you that the difference came. It may be out of our hands. It is true that we know more, and more of each other."

"And you know no harm," said Selina. "Few of us can stand a test. Both of you should have known it."

"Well, I will go and write my manly answer to the letter," said Ninian, in another tone, tossing the envelope into the fire as he passed. "I must get it done, and turn to the future. After all, the prospect is familiar."

Selina waited for the door to close.

"So she wants more than she is worth! Then she may seek it somewhere else. There is no one here to give it."

"'Are we sure it is over?" said Lavinia.

"Father is sure. We can see it," said Egbert. "You the most clearly, unless you are too closely involved."

"And her words were plain," said Hugo.

"You did not see them," said Selina.

"No, but we can guess what they were."

"We feel there is a blank," said Egbert. "Can it come from the loss of Teresa?"

"No," said his sister. "It comes from the loss she has caused. And it has come to stay."

54

"Not in the form you think," said her grandmother. "It will change and take another. Things alter as we live with them. Even this is already different."

"Father will get older," said Lavinia. "And this has been too real to him to come again. But I shall know it is in him to do the same thing in the same way. I go back to him because anything is better than nothing, because I cannot choose. I can't explain my feeling. I see him differently now. It all seems out of my control."

"All feeling is," said Hugo. "Or we should not like people in spite of ourselves, as we are known to. I suppose it is what you are doing."

"Am I to be with Father in the old way, Grandma?" said Lavinia, in a tone that came from the past.

"In what will appear the old way. You will really imitate the old, and so make a new one. I will only tell you what is true."

"I wish we had never seen or heard of Teresa," said Egbert.

"I am not quite sure," said Hugo. "I cannot help loving experience. Even though it is unfortunate, as it always seems to be. I am supposed not to have had any. But I am a person who would be misunderstood."

"I shall always avoid it," said Egbert. "I begin to see what it is. This glimpse is a warning. I feel Lavinia has been sacrificed to me. Of course I don't mean I think I matter. I know too well what I am."

"I have learned it," said Lavinia. "Or rather I have been taught."

"Of course I feel Ninian's troubles as if they were mine," said Hugo. "And I have told you how it is."

"My poor son, his life has not gone well," said Selina. "A mother cannot make up to him. I do not deceive myself."

"That is what I have done," said Lavinia. "And what I shall try to do again. For me there is only one thing."

"You sound as if you were a woman grown," said her grandmother, with a smile.

"I wonder if it will be decided what I am, before there is no longer any doubt."

Selina rose and rustled from the room, with an air of resigned purpose. She went up to the schoolroom and stood just within it, her eyes fixed almost fiercely upon its occupants.

"Agnes and Hengist and Leah, lend me your ears. I come to bury something, not to praise it. The mistake your father has made will not live after him. I have come to end it with a word. It is a word you will hear in silence, with your eyes fixed on my face. Do not look at each other. Do not utter a syllable or a sound. Your father is not going to be married. He will be a widower, as he has always been. The reasons are not for you to seek. And you will not seek them. Do you hear and understand?"

There was silence.

"Should you not answer your grandmother?" said Miss Starkie, in a rather faint tone.

"She said we were not to speak," said Leah.

"He can't always have been a widower," said Hengist. "No one could begin by being that."

"As long as you can remember," said Miss Starkie. "Always, as far as you are concerned."

"Leah, did you hear me?" said Selina, not looking at her grandson.

"Why should I be the one not to hear? Is it our fault that Father is not going to be married? I mean, is it because of us? Didn't she like his having children?"

"She might not have liked his having Lavinia," said Hengist.

"Hengist and Leah, the reasons are not for you to seek."

"We can't help our thoughts. And it seems it is because of us. She must have liked Father for himself."

"She!" just uttered Miss Starkie, not raising her eyes.

"Children, do you understand plain words?"

"Well, we know what they mean," said Hengist. "But we don't always understand. Is it a good thing that Father will always be a widower? It doesn't sound as if it was."

Selina looked at Miss Starkie and heaved a sigh.

"You must have understood that you were not to ask questions," said the latter.

"Or have they no understanding?" breathed the grandmother.

"We shall have to know more," said Leah. "Perhaps Father will tell us."

"Leah, you will not ask him. He is not to be harassed by your questions. You will be silent as the grave."

"We shall not ask him anything. I only said he might tell us."

"Leah, he will tell you nothing. The subject will not be broached."

"It sounds as if there was something wrong about it," said Hengist.

"What does *broach* mean?" said Leah.

"Leah, it means what you are to know it means. That the silence will not be mooted, that there will be silence upon it."

"Why do you keep saying our names?" said Hengist. "We know whom you are speaking to."

"Is *moot* a real word?" said Leah.

"Come, I think you understand your grandmother," said Miss Starkie.

"If they do not, Miss Starkie, will you force my meaning into their heads by any method known? Can I rely on its being battered into them?"

"I think you may depend on me, Mrs. Middleton."

"And I will help, Grandma," said Agnes. "They listen to what I say."

Selina went to the door, signed sternly to Hengist to open it, and passed from sight.

57

"Well, I was not proud of you," said Miss Starkie.

"Were you proud of Grandma?" said Hengist. "We were better than she was. And we oughtn't to be better than an old person."

"It is not for you to criticise your elders."

"We have to criticise Grandma," said Leah. "You would yourself, if you were not in her power."

"My dealings are with your father. And it is her opinion of you that matters. I don't know what she can have thought of you."

"Why don't you know? It was not a secret. It was mooted."

"And if you are not careful, Leah, it will not be a secret from your father," said Selina's voice. "He will know the whole, and will never think the same of you."

"I don't know what he thinks of me now," said Leah to her brother. "So it wouldn't make much difference."

Selina went down to her family, took a seat by the fire, and turned a benevolent eye on them.

"Have you done me the service I asked of you?" said Ninian.

"Yes, it is behind. It was a trivial scene. You need not give a thought to it."

"Nothing is trivial to me," said Hugo. "Let us give it a little thought."

"I am willing to envisage it," said Ninian. "Were the children surprised?"

"I don't know what they were. It does not mean or matter much!"

"Was Miss Starkie surprised?" said Hugo.

"I don't know," said Selina, sounding surprised herself by this line of interest. "It is not her concern. And we never know what children feel, or if they feel anything."

"I wonder your grandchildren like you as much as they do."

"I have felt the same wonder," said Ninian.

"They may know I am sound at heart," said Selina with her lips grave.

"But how can they know? There would have to be some signs."

"Well, we know what true instincts children and animals have. You must have heard about it. It is observant to couple them together."

"They have in the books," said Ninian. "But have they outside them? I should hardly have thought anything about children was sound. They seem so aloof and egoistic."

"More than we can be?" said Egbert.

"You mean you found me such things? You can feel I went through a crisis. And you can hope it did not go deep."

"I hope indeed it did not, Father," said Egbert, gravely.

"We should be thinking of you, Mother," said Ninian. "We forget you have not our strength."

"Yes, the time has come to remember. And it will soon be over. You should not let it pass. I may be better than is thought."

"So may many of us," said Hugo. "Some of us feel we are."

"Do we?" said Lavinia. "I should hardly have said so. We alone know our hidden selves."

"They may be good as well as bad."

"I did not mean the good ones. I don't think they are hidden. People are said to be ashamed of their better qualities. But they seem to face the exposure. Or how do we know they are there? And that there is anything to be ashamed of?"

"You talk as if you were fifty," said Ninian, and broke off at the reminders in his words.

"I can return to my real self, Father. I am glad not to have to act another. I think I may say so once."

"It is well that someone is glad of what has happened."

"That is not what Lavinia said, Father," said Egbert.

"Mother, you must be tired," said Ninian. "I have never seen you so pale."

"I hurried up the staircase to the schoolroom. It is a thing I must not do again. I must forget them both. And one will be glad to be forgotten."

"You must forget the first. You must have the room off the hall. The other you will not forget."

"I am eighty-seven. I married late. I am an old mother for my sons. People say I do not look my age. That shows they realise the age I am. And if I did not look it, I should have a duller face than I have. I watch it in the glass as often as I did in my youth. Where there are fewer marks of time, time must have held less. And I am willing for it to hold more. I would rather be alive then dead. When I die, people will say it is the best thing for me. It is because they know it is the worst. They want to avoid the feeling of pity. As though they were the people most concerned!"

"Well, it is very dreadful to feel pity," said Hugo.

"And I don't believe in a future life, or want to. I should not like any form of it I know. I don't want to be a spirit or to return to the earth as someone else. I could never like anyone else enough for that."

"And we are irritated by other people," said Lavinia. "Suppose we were irritated by the people we were! As we never are, it seems to disprove the theory."

"I don't know I shan't hear your talk, when I am dead. An after life might also have that drawback. There is little good in being out of things and knowing it."

"You would be supposed to be in so many more," said Ninian.

"But only in a comfortless, disembodied way," said Lavinia. "Think how we conceive of ghosts, when we accept them. I hardly like to think of it as applying to Grandma."

"I think chains and headlessness are incurred by those who fall short in life," said Selina, not shrinking from this

60

length herself. "Or were the victims of those who did."

"It is odd that believers visualise spirits in that way. When you think how they should imagine them."

"It shows it is impossible to believe," said Egbert.

"Or rare to have reason," said Ninian.

"You allow the children to believe, Grandma," said Lavinia.

"They need to accept an All-seeing Eye. Or rather we need them to. No ordinary eye could embrace their purposes. We may as well depute what we can."

"Even to an imaginary overseer," said Ninian. "And in fairness to Miss Starkie."

"Is not retribution too far away to count?" said Hugo.

"No doubt," said Selina. "But the idea of being watched is discouraging. I found it so."

"You are thinking of the two little ones," said Ninian.

"It may also be true of Agnes, but I think less."

"I should not have thought she would be your favourite. Though I have seen she is. The others are more your type."

"That may be the reason. I like ordinary children. And of course I can't think I was that. And looking back, I don't much like myself."

"People generally pity themselves, when they look back."

"And I daresay you are among them. But I don't want to hear about it. It is too late to remedy the matter. And I am not as concerned for your early days as for my last ones. Childhood is not the only time that calls for pity."

"You are a heroic figure, Mother, and naturally proud of it."

"Things we are proud of are seldom an advantage to us," said Lavinia. "Unless we ought not to be proud of them. And then they may be a great one."

"Agnes and Hengist and Leah!" said Selina, deepening her voice. "What are you doing in the hall? Is it your schoolroom?"

"It is for the moment, Mrs. Middleton," said Miss

61

Starkie from the doorway. "I was calling their attention to the panelling. It is of an unusual design."

"Why do you not open the door and come in?" said Selina, her voice hardly veiling suggestion of social shortcoming.

Miss Starkie remained where she was, and looked behind her, as though her concern was here.

"Come in and speak to your grandmother," she said, admitting a faint sigh into her tone.

"Do you want us, Grandma?" said Agnes.

"Should I call you, if I did not? I asked what you were doing in the hall."

"You know, now she has told you," said Hengist.

Miss Starkie smiled at Ninian, but at no one else.

"Your patience should abash them, Miss Starkie. It would serve them right, if it failed."

"Ah, but how much would fail with it, Mr. Middleton! How much effort would be wasted! I shall win in the end. Never fear."

"I admit to some doubt," said Hugo.

"Ah, I do not, Mr. Hugo. Wild horses would not drag the admission from me."

"Wild horses never have much success," said Lavinia. "Their history is a record of failure. And we do suggest a good deal for them."

CHAPTER V

"Can you hear me, Mother?" said Ninian.

"Yes, of course. I am not dead."

"We hope you are not going to die."

"That might go without saying."

"You know it does," said Hugo.

"It did not," said Selina, wearily.

"Do you want to say anything, Mother?"

"No, I don't want a deathbed scene. When it is acted, it means nothing. And why should I consider my last moments? The others have done more for me."

"And it is so terrible of them to be the last," murmured Hugo.

"All of them count to us," said Ninian. "We need not tell you how much."

"We need not call up memories. I cannot carry them with me."

"You will leave them with us," said Hugo.

"Well, I have been as good to you as you have to me. And better to the son who has left me."

"We have nothing to regret," said Ninian.

"He will find enough when I cannot know about it. And it will do nothing for either of us."

"The word need not exist between you and me."

"If I die, you will find some reason for it. But it will pass."

"You don't sound as if you are going to die," said Hugo.

"No," said Selina, almost smiling. "And I can see the nurse agrees. She feels I am not fit for a higher life; and I would choose the lower one. And she thinks I should be afraid to die."

63

"And you are afraid of nothing," said her son.

"I don't feel I am going to meet my Maker. And if I were, I should not fear him. He has not earned the feeling. I almost think he ought to fear me."

"I think he must," murmured Hugo. "She seems so much her usual self."

"It may be coming back," said Selina. "The doctor is not sure."

"He has not said anything to you?"

"How can he, when there is nothing to say? And when he sees I know it."

"Would you like to see the children?" said Ninian. "I mean it might make a change for you."

"I know what you might have meant. You should take more care. I know all I want to about them. It might hardly be a suitable moment to know the whole."

"They need not know—we need not tell them you are ill."

"They would not mind. It could only mean I might die."

"You know how they would feel about that."

"I believe I do. And I can't explain it," said Selina, almost petulantly.

"They feel your bark is worse than your bite."

"That is an empty saying. Only bark has a place in life. There is no opportunity to bite. I have wished there was."

"They know you would not have used it."

"I am going to sleep," said Selina, and closed her eyes.

"We have not been a success," said Hugo. "Even you did not aim high."

"It would have been to court failure. I chose to avoid it."

"We have met it on a meaner scale. And she saw the meanness."

"Yes, I saw it," said Selina, dreamily.

As the pair went out of the room, they were noiselessly approached by Ainger.

64

"How is the mistress to-day, sir?"

"Very ill, as you know," said Ninian. "Her heart is weak."

"I can't help feeling she is more herself," said Hugo.

"Well, neither can I, sir. I have the intimation."

"I think you might have it, if you heard her talk."

"Yes, sir, that might support it," said Ainger, who had found it did.

"You will see the hall is kept quiet?" said Ninian.

"Yes, sir. That accounts for my presence. Otherwise there are calls on my time."

"When the post comes, do not take any letters to the mistress. One of us will take them later."

"Yes, sir. Miss Lavinia sorts the second post. It can be left to her," said Ainger, as the two men moved away.

"Well, has anything transpired, Ainger?" said another voice.

"Well, I have my impression, Cook. And Mr. Hugo shared it."

"And what did you share? Words are at your disposal."

"Well, I was on guard here to prevent disturbance. And I could not help hearing what passed."

"I believe you cannot help it, Ainger," said Cook gravely. "And it is time you conquered yourself. You will be hearing something to cause discomfiture."

"For myself or somebody else?"

"Well, who was in the uncertain place? And is it a case for insinuation?"

"You are right, Cook. It is not the occasion. And I was not about to go further. But I chanced to hear the mistress, that is, to catch her words."

"I throw no doubt on it. I fear it is the truth. And they acted as a check on you?"

"Well, perhaps that was hardly the case," said Ainger, controlling a smile.

"Well, explain yourself. There is no call to be oracular."

"To tell you the truth, Cook," said Ainger, lowering

his voice and leaning towards her, "if I were on the brink, as the mistress may be, I should not feel such words of a kind to pass my lips."

"Why, they were not of a dubious nature?"

"Cook, if they were, should I pass them on? Should I betray a lady on the verge, and of an age and standing?"

"I hope not, Ainger. I go no further. And what are you doing?"

"Well, I have done it now," said Ainger, changing his tone. "And it was not so much. Just her tendency, if you understand."

"I do, Ainger. And the Almighty might do so too, having fashioned her as she is."

"Well, in his place I should feel I might have done better. What is the good of being almighty?"

"It is not a place you would be in. And you may continue in another vein."

"Well, there is more to come, if I am to tell the whole. But perhaps my lips should be sealed."

"If it may fester, Ainger, if it may act in that way, you should cast it off. There are things that are better shared."

"You said the Almighty would understand the mistress, as he had fashioned her. I wonder what he would say to his existence being questioned. Who would have fashioned her then?"

"Surely it was not what passed?"

"Cook, it was implied. The after life was doubted. And in a light spirit."

"Well, she goes to what is before her. We do not penetrate further. It might be too much."

"It might indeed in a sense."

"Ainger, we will say no more. It is not our part to frame thoughts."

"I don't think the old lady will leave us myself. And we may feel it to be as well."

"Myself I say one thing. I have had kindness from the mistress. Those remain my words."

66

"You might say other things, if you heard what I do."

"Ainger, you lower yourself. Listening is your snare. You carry it beyond a point. And here are the postman and Miss Lavinia; they warn us that we are wasting time."

"One letter for the mistress, two for the master, one each for you and Mr. Egbert, miss," said Ainger. "One for Cook, if I may take it. And none for your humble servant; I mean none for me, miss. Well, it saves the need of reply."

"Don't you like writing letters?" said Lavinia.

"Well, when I attain the mood, miss. Then the words out-distance my pen," said Ainger, as he strode away.

"Any letters for me?" said Egbert, entering the hall.

"One each for you and me and Father," said Lavinia, putting the last on the table. "Here are yours and mine. I will take Grandma's to her room."

"Will she be able to read it?"

"Well, it may be the last. And then what a home it will be! Grandma gone, Father gone in spirit, no change in anything else! We shall spend our lives waiting for a difference that does not come."

Lavinia went in to Selina's room, and as she came out met Ninian.

"There is a letter for you in the hall, Father. I have put one by Grandma's bed. She seemed to see and hear me. I wonder how often she will do either again."

"I can't help feeling she is better. She seemed so like herself."

"She will be that as long as she breathes. It is not in her to be different."

"When we are near our end, there must seem to be less in us. It is not so with her. It may mean she has not reached it."

"If only it could mean it, Father!"

Ninian put his hand on her shoulder, and they went together to the library. Her face was resolute and somehow uplifted, and his quiet and without hope. When they sat down, he put his arm about her in his old way, and she leant against him in hers. Egbert and Hugo looked at them, and at each other; and the old life seemed to return as a shadow of itself.

It was not many days before Selina was amongst them, weak and on a sofa, but alert to all that passed.

"How angry I feel," said Egbert, "that we have suffered needless anxiety! And what a foolish word it is! As if anxiety did any good!"

"It has done some in this case," said Selina. "It has enhanced my value."

"It has made us realise it, Mother," said Ninian.

"I will make the most of it. I am in no hurry for the usual round. And there is no need for what I do. I will just see my letters and answer those that want it."

"There were not very many," said Lavinia. "It is too soon for you to trouble. None of them would be urgent. There is none for you to-day, Uncle Hugo."

"How kind to make it sound an exception! I am sorry not to have one to-day."

"You had several a week or two ago," said Egbert.

"Whom were they from?" said Selina.

"Oh, no one who mattered," said Hugo.

"Don't baffle me, my boy. Why should I suffer curiosity? You have letters so seldom."

"Why should I suffer mortification? How do you know I have not a clandestine correspondence?"

"Perhaps it is what you were having," said Lavinia, smiling.

"Were the letters from Teresa?" said Ninian.

"Yes. It was almost as Lavinia says. It was a covert interchange, and brought matters to a close. I betrayed what I was, in time. And she saw what I was not. And all was as if it had not been."

"So it was as I knew," said Selina. "Well, I always know."

"So a chapter is ended," said Lavinia.

"This was hardly a page," said Hugo.

"Unlike my part of it," said Ninian. "I will not deny the truth."

"It was all the same one, Father. It is closed now."

"I wonder what she saw in you, Hugo," said Selina. "I suppose mothers always wonder that."

"I thought they saw what no one else could see."

"You showed the best of yourself. And she took you at your valuation. That is what people do."

"Only because we hope so. They really take us at theirs. And that is what she came to do. Mine was a little different."

"It is a common position," said Egbert. "We do tend to feel we might be taken at a higher one. Think how Miss Starkie must feel it."

"I daresay she does. Indeed I have seen signs of it," said Selina, as if this was not in Miss Starkie's favour.

"She has no reason to hide them," said Ninian.

"She only does her duty. She is in as good a place as she deserves."

"As good as has come her way. She deserves a kingdom."

"And she has one, Mr. Middleton," said Miss Starkie's voice. "Her own little kingdom of youth and hope, the kingdom of her choice. And she would not change it. Her own view of it is enough for her."

"That is a happy thing for us. Can we help you in it?"

"I came for some reassurance for the children about their grandmother," said Miss Starkie, her tone light on the last word, as though not bestowing on it any deep feeling. "Agnes has been in great—has been quite anxious about her."

"And no one else anything at all," said Selina. "If I had died, Leah would have said it made no difference. And Hengist would not have disputed it."

"Oh, I think Leah uses those words in a sense of her own."

69

"I don't doubt she does. With the simplest meaning."

"She is limited to her range. She does not yet deal in the wider issues. Oh, there is a great deal of good hidden in Leah."

"I don't see how we are to know about it."

"It will emerge in time. We need have no fear. I have none. Deep things grow slowly."

"I don't know why they should. Or how we know they are deep."

"Oh, I believe you have a soft spot in your heart for Leah, Mrs. Middleton," said Miss Starkie, using her own powers of divination.

"It is to my credit, if I have. There is nothing to help me. Unless your faith is infectious."

"Ah, I believe it is. I believe it is gaining a hold. I see the signs."

"Well, tell the children their grandmother is almost herself," said Ninian. "And thank you for coming to see."

"I rejoice—shall be glad to be the bearer of such tidings. And, if I may, I will say she is quite herself. I see every sign of it. Thank you, Egbert."

Miss Starkie smiled and passed through the door, and Selina rose.

"She reminds us that things must go on. It is a quality in her calling. I will go and deal with my letters. I have not looked at them."

"No, don't go yourself, Grandma," said Lavinia, getting up. "I will fetch them, and you can sort them here. There are only a few."

"I will go," said Egbert. "The lid of that desk is stiff. I remember how to deal with it."

"No, I will go," said his sister, moving past him and checking herself. "It must be opened in a certain way. In one place the wood is broken."

"Let Egbert go," said Ninian. "You don't need to do everything, Lavinia."

His daughter sat down and opened a book, and her

brother returned with the letters and gave them to his grandmother.

"Not so many," she said. "I was not ill long. Some from people who do not matter. They are the ones who write. I suppose we mean less to the others. No need to answer them yet. It keeps the ball rolling. A letter without an envelope, that must have got in by mistake. Dated ten days ago, when I was at my worst. It is for you, Ninian, and from Teresa! Now how is that explained?"

"You must have opened it when you were ill, and hardly knew what you were doing. You thought it would trouble me, and put it out of sight. Your mind was out of control. That is what it must have been."

"Or anyhow might have been," said Lavinia.

"But was not. My mind was my own, when I used it. I should have thought you would remember. I did not open letters or put them anywhere. I should not have done either."

"Of course you would not, Grandma; or not consciously," said Lavinia.

"The letter would have been addressed to Father," said Egbert. "And would normally have been put in the hall."

"Unless it was enclosed in a letter to Grandma," said Lavinia.

"That is an idea," said her father. "That may be what it was. Teresa did not want a letter in her writing to be about. And there were reasons against it."

"But where is the letter to me? And where are the envelopes?" said Selina. "I have none of them. And I opened nothing."

"You may have forgotten," said her son. "It is best not to think about it."

He sent his eyes down to the letter, as if he could not keep them from it.

"What does it say, Father?" said Lavinia, in a tentative tone.

71

Ninian did not answer, and in a moment spoke almost to himself.

"So her word came and miscarried. It might not have come to light. How we are in the hands of chance!"

"In the hands of something else," said Selina. "Chance is not equal to so much. I hold to what I have said. I was conscious or not all the time. There was no middle state."

"That is the one that is not recognised by the person who is in it."

"It is recognised by other people, indeed imagined by them. But it can serve its purpose. Let it all be as you say. We will leave it there."

"Does the letter matter, Father?" said Lavinia, just uttering the words.

"It tells me something I was meant to know. Its coming to me late may matter. But I can hope not."

"What does it say, my son?" said Selina.

"I was waiting for that. Do you expect me to read it aloud?"

"Not if it is only for yourself. You can give it to me later."

"I will keep it in my own hands," said Ninian.

"Does it say anything we are to know?" said Hugo.

"Well, it throws its light. On you and herself. It may be I, who lose the chance to appear as I am."

"Let us hear it, if you can, Father," said Lavinia. "It is the simplest way."

Her father glanced at her and opened the letter.

" 'Dear Ninian,

I have a word to say to you, more honest than most women would say. I have now little feeling for my own life. The one I thought I had, has gone, as such feelings have gone before. So I have little to give, and little zest for giving it. But I will give it to you, if it is better than nothing for you. If it is not, do not answer this letter, and in a week I will put you and yours in a memory to be uncovered only by myself. Yours with regret and remembrance,

Teresa Chilton.' "

"Well, that is her offer," said Selina. "So you may have what is left."

"It has its own quality," said Lavinia. "She has little to give, and so offers little. She does not evade the truth."

"She offers all she has," said Ninian. "I offered no more."

"It seems a shadow of a letter, Father. It somehow has no substance."

"It means what it does, as you have said."

"Yes, we must give her her due. She is ending things as well as she can. Perhaps she could not do less. But she could not do more either."

"I still do not want anyone's opinion of her."

"It is only mine, Father; not the same to you as any other," said Lavinia, putting her hand on his. "And we share it, as we share everything."

Ninian covered the hand with his own, but answered without looking at her.

"We will share what we can. Some things are only for ourselves."

"I wish everything was," said Hugo at once. "It is the first feeling I remembered. I was glad to grow up and no longer be reproached for it."

"I feel the same," said Egbert. "I love things to be all mine."

"I am the opposite," said his sister. "Nothing means anything without the further meaning."

"What kind of things are you talking of?" said Selina.

"Of everything," said Lavinia, lifting her hands. "Of feelings, thoughts, hopes, mistakes, troubles and joys, everything."

"I did not know we were talking of so much," said Ninian.

73

"Teresa writes like a man," said Egbert, looking at the letter.

"I have noticed that," said Selina. "I have thought her a little like a man in herself."

"I should have said she was the pure feminine," said Lavinia. "Herself and all to do with her. I don't remember her writing. I don't mean anything against her."

"Why should you?" said Ninian. "What are you but feminine yourself?"

"Oh, not purely, Father. Either in myself or as I have been influenced. It is quite a different thing."

"Well, something is different."

"We think of a masculine woman as tall and strong," said Egbert. "Teresa is neither."

"I did not mean masculine in that sense," said Selina.

"You don't know what you mean, Grandma," said Lavinia, smiling.

"I know what she meant," said Ninian. "I have thought it myself."

"Perhaps that is why Uncle Hugo could not meet her— her hopes, her instincts—we need not know what they were. There was not the attraction of opposites."

"In your view there would have been."

"If she had succeeded—met what she wished, we would have welcomed her in the new character."

"That was hardly the issue of the matter for them."

"I wonder why we talk so much about her."

"It was natural, after the letter came to light."

"Well it alters nothing, as you would not have answered it. You could only have been silent, as she seemed to know."

"One difference is that I did not have the choice."

"Cannot we leave the matter?" said Hugo. "You must know how embarrassed I am by it."

"We are held by the human story," said Egbert. "It is really better than a book."

"It has not been a deep one," said Lavinia. "And it is ended now."

"Your opinion does not alter it, and neither does mine," said Ninian. "But they are not the same."

"Marry her, if you want to, my son," said Selina. "It is what she would choose."

"I do want to," said Ninian, with a cry in his voice. "I want her presence, her companionship, the stake in the future. I will have it, if I can."

There was a short silence.

"Then answer the letter, Father," said Lavinia, in an urgent tone. "You may be in time. Do not let any passing uncertainty blight the hopes of your life. I will come and help you to put the answer into words."

"No, I will do it myself," said Ninian, going to the door. "But thank you, my dear. I hoped you would not fail me. I am glad you have not."

"So the letter does its work!" said Egbert. "Suppose it had not been found!"

"It is as well that it has," said Lavinia. "We must say it now. It was written to be read, and it has met its fate. As Father's stepping-stone to happiness it must be accepted. More, it must be welcomed! It is the only thing."

"So the change is to come," said Selina. "I have only to be a witness of it. It is not the first time for me."

"What shall I do?" said Hugo. "Stay in the house, or go?"

"Stay with me, my boy. I may need you. I must partly lose one son."

"I was thinking of Teresa."

"You need not be troubled there. A woman so placed would not turn to the man again."

" 'Hell holds no fury'—" said Lavinia.

"There is nothing of that kind. We have heard the truth. And it is better that the change should come. It ends the threat of it. We shall soon accustom ourselves. And the habit may be as hard to break as any other."

75

"How much wisdom you have, Grandma! I hope we can depend on it."

"I have had time to gain it, and give it trial. You can have it too, if you accept it. There are things that do the work of time."

Selina held out her hand, and her grand-daughter moved towards it, drew up short and ran out of the room.

"Poor child!" said Selina. "And poor old woman!"

"Poor man!" said Hugo, indicating himself.

"Poor youth!" said Egbert.

"Poor Ninian!" said Selina. "That is where the doubt lies. For the rest of us there is none. Go to your sister, my boy. You can be of help, and should be happy to know it."

Egbert went up to Lavinia's room and found her sitting by the window.

"It is cold in here," he said. "The sun has gone."

"Gone for ever," she said, with a smile to make light of her words. "It will not come out again."

"Whoever put that letter in the desk, did sorry work. What was the point of opening it, if it was to be put where it would be found?"'

"I suppose it would have been wrong to destroy it."

"It was wrong to open it. When that was done, the thing might have been carried to its end."

"He felt it was the lesser guilt to stop half-way. *He* we say. We seem to think it was a man. And it seems a man's idea."

"What man can it have been? Hardly Ainger; the thought is beyond him; and he was too little involved. And Uncle would have gone the whole way."

"We can think of motives for Uncle, I suppose."

"Or of motives for me. Or even more for you. But let us pursue the truth. The letter was to be found, and found too late. The full result with half the guilt. That might be a line of thought."

"Perhaps it was a case of curiosity. That might lead

76

to hiding the letter. And it gives us a wider range. It was a trivial gain for the risk involved. But wrong-doers may not reason. They would hardly be a high type."

"We are all wrong-doers," said Egbert. "We cannot argue from that. Did he think that Grandma would die, and that the guilt would be ascribed to her?"

"After her death? When she could not deny it? What a pleasing thought!"

"Too base for Uncle Hugo. We must turn elsewhere."

"We should stop this pursuit of everyone. We shall find ourselves hounding each other."

"I will tell you my final suspicion. As with Father, it rests on Grandma. The letter came into her hands by mistake, and she read it and hid it in the desk. She would have recognised the writing. You remember she spoke of it. Father thought she did it when she was not herself. Or perhaps he hoped so. I incline to think she was herself all the while. And the time came when she could ease her conscience."

"Guilty people have such tender ones. Well, in either case she is the person to choose. We will leave it there. And we will not trouble her about it. She is in no fit state. And it was rather heroic of her."

"Why could not Teresa manage better? It is her uncertainties that have brought us to the pass. I wonder if Uncle tried to save us, and is guilty after all."

"We must not go on. It will end nowhere. And the other idea is more plausible."

"Do you hope that Father will be in time with his answer?"

"What can I do, as things are? If he hopes it, so must I. And he has been living apart from us. We can let ourselves see it now. A new life may be no worse than an imitation of the old one."

"We can't know what it will be. There are worse things than a copy."

"There are honester things. Unless the copy is a faithful one."

There was a knock at the door, and Hugo entered with an openly shamefaced air.

"I am in great discomfiture. I know the guilt is mine."

"Yours?" said Egbert. "And we were suspecting Grandma! Why did your heart fail you?"

"We don't blame Grandma," said Lavinia. "She will not hear a word from us. You need not fear."

"Oh! Of course I should like to be shielding a woman and admiring myself. But I did not mean the letter. I meant I ought to have responded to Teresa. Thinking of myself has never done so much harm. It generally does so much less than I expect."

"Did she propose to you?" said Lavinia.

"No, she only thought I should propose to her. I think it is a thing she is used to. And then she began to be afraid of it. I will not misrepresent her. So you were ready to see me as the culprit of the letter. And I do see that perhaps I ought to have been."

"It had to be someone," said Egbert. "That was the truth before us. We could not shut our eyes to it, and we faced it with courage. And with many of our other human qualities. We told you where our choice fell. On a person you must not judge."

"No, a man speaks no evil of his mother. And it must have gone against the grain. She has hidden nothing in her life. Not even her thought."

"Well, not that," said Lavinia, smiling. "And not her action to the end. Not long enough for it to do its work. Though she may have thought she had. Well, whatever happens, you will stay with us?"

"Yes, what is the reason for my going? The matter is nothing to Teresa, of course. And I can't afford to be anywhere else. And I persuade myself that my place is at your side."

"I shall welcome your presence in many situations."

"There should not be such things. They ought to be forbidden."

"I shall not try to make them. You need not fear."

"I did fear a little. I do judge people by myself. And they are often very like me."

"Lavinia is like none of us," said Egbert. "She is on her own plane."

"Well, Father is too much to me, for me to spoil his happiness."

"You have no ignoble instincts," said Hugo. "So you don't have to give your life to suppressing them. It can be a great burden. Perhaps it is why I have done nothing else."

"I have too many. But to yield would mean more loss than gain."

"Even if you gained your father?"

"I should have lost myself," said Lavinia.

"I have never thought about losing myself. I will think now. I do feel I am worth keeping."

"We should all feel it. It is what makes us ourselves. And the new life has to come. It is some time since it actually came."

"You are the person who ought to have hidden the letter."

"So I am," said Lavinia, laughing. "I can't help feeling for the person who did it. I have never felt so lenient towards what we must call a base action."

"Must we, if it was done by your grandmother?"

"If we call it anything. But we need not talk of it, and will not. It must be forgotten."

"It was a great change to come at her age," said Egbert. "If she could not face it, we should hardly blame her. Again at her age."

"I suppose we must blame her, if she knew what she was doing," said Lavinia, gravely. "But we will feel she did not."

"What interest there is in the future!" said Hugo. "It takes so little to enthral me."

"A certain amount, if this is an example," said Egbert.

"And why is it called short? Even a day has no end. Think of the one we are living."

"Oh, let us forget it, and everything about it," said Lavinia. "And never remember it again. It has been a disordered day."

CHAPTER VI

"Is she really married to Father this time?" said Leah.

"Now what am I to say?" said Miss Starkie. "Yes, of course she is."

"So she said *she*," said Hengist.

"So she will always be here now," said Agnes.

"Well, I really don't know what word you are to use," said Miss Starkie.

"What is the good of words that mustn't be used?" said Hengist. "*She* isn't different from any other."

"It seems it must be," said Miss Starkie. "I don't know what we should have done without it."

"You are not often on our side," said Leah.

"I am always on it. You must be told what you need to know."

"You don't know this yourself."

"I don't pretend to," said Miss Starkie. "Now be ready to welcome your father and—Mrs. Middleton, when they come."

"Mrs. Middleton is Grandma," said Leah.

"Your stepmother. She takes your father's name now."

"Why doesn't he take hers?"

"It is not the custom. The man is the head of the family."

"He isn't really," said Hengist. "I suppose, if she liked, we should all be called Chilton."

"She is Mrs. Middleton," said Miss Starkie, and said no more.

"I think *she* is really best," said Leah.

"Well, you prove your opinion. Now be ready to greet—the travellers when they come. Seem to be glad to see them. Now here is the moment."

"Well, we are with you again," said Ninian. "Ready to resume our place and our powers. I hope you are resolved to support us."

"It isn't resuming for *her*," said Hengist. "He talks in the plural like a royal person."

"Well, he has the power," said Leah.

"I am not going to say anything," said Miss Starkie.

"Are you what is called at the end of your tether?"

"Yes, I am."

"So you did say something."

Miss Starkie did not add to it, and Ninian continued.

"Our three generations are complete. I am no longer a solitary figure. The gap in our ranks is filled."

"They are not complete," said Leah. "Grandma hasn't a husband. And she and Father aren't a real husband and wife."

"Don't be foolish; of course they are," said Miss Starkie.

"What did she say?" said Teresa, smiling at Leah.

"Nothing worth repeating, Mrs. Middleton. There is much to be said for the old ideas about children. I am often tempted to act on them."

"Yield to the temptation," said Ninian. "It is not one to be resisted."

"She will want to see her room," said Agnes. "Shall I take her to it?"

"Now there is a thing to be said," said Ninian. "The name is to be *Teresa* for the two elder ones, and *Mamma* for the rest. So now there will be no question."

"So you have simply to remember," said Miss Starkie. "And nothing more need be said."

"It will be easier for you, Miss Starkie," said Ninian.

"It will open up a new era, Mr. Middleton. I shall not dare to look back on the last one."

"What is an era?" said Leah.

"A historical period. I used the word ironically. Now we will talk of something else."

82

"I suppose *Mamma* is a sort of feeble word for *Mother*?" said Leah, obeying the injunction.

"They mean almost the same. *Mamma* is perhaps a lighter word. Now there is an end of the matter."

"We shan't have so much to talk about," said Hengist.

"You will make the best of what there is."

"How I wish I was not here!" said Hugo to Lavinia. "It is humbling to be forced to stay. And they say poverty is no disgrace. I wonder what put the word into their heads."

"It is best to get the meeting over. Have you spoken to Teresa?"

"I will speak to her at once. I will try to be a man. I will anyhow be an imitation."

Hugo went up to Teresa.

"I suppose you hardly recognise me. I am so different from what you thought. And I forgot to ask if I could be your brother. But it did not matter, as I was to become so anyhow. This will do for our first word. I could not leave it to you."

"Not if I could not recognise you. Now I shall be able to."

"You will see me as I am. I am always seen in that way. I have had to get used to it. I am grateful to you for trying to see me differently. I have had something in my life. It is more than I expected."

"We do usually have less. But many of us expect too much. We hardly like to remember what it was."

"What is the best thing to have?" said Egbert. "We are told it is not wealth and ease. I suppose for fear we should think it was. It is sad how we understand it."

"Anyone who does not, is without understanding," said Selina. "I don't mean that I should choose it."

"You would not dare to mean it," said Hugo. "I almost believe I should. The best thing about wealth is that it is never shared."

"It ought to be," said Lavinia.

"That almost seems to make it better."

"The good thing about it is the power to share it."

"But a better one is that the power is not used."

"I suppose it is not. It is a hard thing to explain."

"I hardly think it is," said Ninian. "Wealth is the thing that can be shared. We cannot share looks or gifts or charm. I daresay we should not, if we could. If we had them, I mean."

"Oh, of course you mean that, Father," said Lavinia, laughing.

"None of us likes to be copied," said Egbert. "And I suppose that is trying to share."

"Trying to steal," said his grandmother.

"I have always known they were the same," said Hugo.

"We have not settled on the best thing in life," said Lavinia.

"Human friendship?" said Egbert.

"But it is sometimes shared," said Hugo.

"And it is uncertain," said Teresa. "We want something we cannot lose."

"A clear conscience?" said Ninian.

"We can surely lose that," said Lavinia, continuing at once. "Not that many of us do in any real sense."

"I should have thought we all did," said Hugo. "Perhaps that shows it is the best. We should naturally lose that."

"Real achievement?" said Selina.

"But we don't know a case of it," said Lavinia. "So we can't ask if it is the best. And anyhow no one would dare to answer."

"It depends what kind of achievement you mean," said Teresa.

"Not service to humanity," said Hugo. "No one could feel that the best."

"Some people might," said Lavinia. "Those who could give it."

84

"People with religion," said Egbert. "Who feel they will be rewarded in the end."

"That might be a good thing," said Hugo. "But from what is said of it, I hardly think the best."

"Real achievement would be independent of reward," said Ninian. "The reward would be in itself."

"I knew there was some drawback," said Hugo. "Fancy having to provide the reward as well as earn it!"

"It is said that effort is its own reward," said Lavinia. "Perhaps that is why it often has no other."

"What should we really choose?" said Ninian. "We have not said."

"An affection that would last," said Teresa; "in ourselves as well as in someone else; that would be a basis for our lives."

"That would be my choice," said Lavinia.

"Well, may you both have it," said Selina, in benevolence. "Try to give it to each other."

"It could hardly be done under instruction." said Ninian.

"Affection often lasts," said Hugo. "We don't often have the interest of seeing people lose it. It would always last in me, if they asked it of me. But they might almost think I had none to give."

"Perhaps they might quite think so," said Teresa, in a low tone, with a smile.

"So you can say such a thing to me. I could not to you. I somehow feel I am returning good for evil."

"Does anyone ever do that?" said Selina.

"Not you, Grandma, if you can't believe in it," said Lavinia. "And it is hard to see why anyone should. It may be a sign of weakness."

"It must be," said Egbert. "No one could want to do it."

"People might do it out of their strength," said Teresa.

"I will not imagine them," said Hugo. "I should not dare."

"We might do it for our credit or self-esteem," said Ninian. "Perhaps that should hardly count."

"We should feel the last," said Egbert. "I don't see how it could be avoided."

"What other reasons are there?" said Hugo. "I cannot think of any."

"It is not as plain as you all think," said Lavinia.

"Why, have you personal knowledge or experience?" said Ninian.

"You should not ask dreadful questions," said Hugo. "You deserve to have a dreadful answer."

"He will not have one," said Lavinia. "It would not do for us to meet our deserts."

"So he has had one," said Selina, almost to herself.

"Are we talking of actual evil?" said Ninian, as if he had not heard. "Or of natural effort for our own welfare?"

"Oh, that is almost too evil to speak about," said Hugo. "Some subjects should be forbidden."

"Well, are we to talk about ourselves and each other? Is that a better or safer thing? People might take the chance to speak the truth."

"Only terrible people. But of course that is nearly everyone."

"Is our choice of subjects so small?" said Egbert.

"Well, it is for me," said Hugo. "I only like the personal ones. And no one really seems to introduce any others."

"Then would you like to speak the truth about people?"

"Yes, if I were not afraid to. But I think it is a wholesome fear."

"Why should the truth be against them?" said Lavinia.

"We meant the truth that is spoken about them. That deals with what they think is hidden. And it ought to be hidden no doubt. They are the ones to judge."

"Is it often spoken?" said Teresa. "I suppose when it is forced out of people."

"It is terrible how little force is needed. Our self-knowledge takes us such a long way."

"I don't think I have learned much from mine," said Lavinia.

"It can teach us all a good deal," said her father.

"It might lead us to judge other people by ourselves. And that might make us too gullible."

"That suggests that we are better than they are. And of some of us it may be true."

"It is," said Teresa, looking at Lavinia. "And it is not their fault if they know it."

"My sister understands about the hidden things," said Egbert, "though she herself may not have them."

"They would not remain hidden," said Lavinia, laughing. "In my case they would emerge."

"They would not in mine," said Hugo. "They are far too securely hidden. I hardly dare to recognise them myself. I might betray them."

"I know all about mine. And I fear so do you all. I have not the gift of hiding them."

"Fancy not having to cultivate it! I thought that became our second nature. I did not know we ever showed our first one."

"You are patient with my family," said Ninian to his wife. "They love words for their own sake."

"So do I, when they come from them. But they must not expect them from me. I cannot emulate them."

"You will not try. To emulate may be to copy. That is not for you."

"No, people have to take me as I am."

"As you really are?" said Hugo. "I have only met your case and Lavinia's. There should be a bond between you."

"Perhaps there will be," said Lavinia.

"Not too strong," said Ninian, looking at her. "You both belong to me. That is where the bond lies."

"Fancy daring to ask so much for yourself!" said Hugo.

"The more we ask, the more we have. And it is fair enough: asking is not always easy."

"And it is said to be hard to accept," said Lavinia. "So no wonder we have so little."

" 'Nothing venture, nothing have' is a heartless saying," said Egbert. "Fancy recognising that we may have nothing."

"And we are to value things more when they don't come easily. There is no limit to the heartlessness."

"When we really feel that everything is our due," said Ninian.

"That ought to fill you with humility," said Hugo. "As artists are filled with it, when they are praised."

"Don't they take praise as their due?" said Lavinia. "When they are not praised, they hardly seem filled with humility."

"I suppose it means they are filled with pride," said Teresa.

"Who said she could not use words like any one else?" said Ninian.

"I hope she will not go on doing it," said Hugo. "Another person to put me into the shade!"

"Don't you like the shade?" said Teresa.

"Well, no one is filled with humility to overflowing."

"Now I am going to claim an hour with my wife alone," said Ninian. "That is due to us on our first day."

"As many hours as you like on every day, Father," said Lavinia. "That is why we did not offer them on the first."

"Will you come and share the hour with us?" said Teresa.

"No," said Ninian, at once. "The hour is yours and mine. We will share others later."

"What irony of fate!" said Egbert, looking after them. "The usurper of a place invites her predecessor to share it. Would that lead to less trouble or more?"

"More," said Selina. "It is not a case for sharing. There are very few."

"The very word repels me," said Hugo. "Why should

we not have what is our own? There is no good reason."

"That is Father's feeling," said Egbert. "But Teresa seems to be without it. Perhaps she is a high type. We may meet one too seldom to recognise it."

"Why are types only high and low?" said Hugo. "Cannot an ordinary person belong to them? Or do they only embrace extremes?"

"You can be a mediocre type," said his mother.

"Oh, I am sure I can't. I am sure nobody could. That is why we never hear of one. There is such a thing as going too far."

"Father wants Teresa for himself," said Egbert. "But he can hardly keep her from Lavinia. The feeling has no reason in it."

"It has other things," said Selina.

"You don't mean I am to regard it, Grandma? He should be glad for Teresa to have a friend in me. It would ease the path for them both."

"It might fill it, when he wants it free."

"He is not a man to ask everything for himself."

"No, but he asks one thing."

"The whole of Teresa? She hardly seems to want the whole of him."

"No, that is true. We remember her letter."

"Her letter? Oh, yes he read it to us."

"It was you who asked him to."

"Yes, it was. It seemed best for us to hear it. I remember now."

"It is easy to forget what we have not read ourselves."

"Yes, but we remember the gist of it."

"Perhaps not as well as Grandma does," said Egbert in a whisper.

Lavinia seemed not to hear.

"Agnes!" said Miss Starkie's voice. "What are you doing down here? Why did you not come with the others?"

"You didn't tell me to."

"You knew I meant all three of you."

89

"I don't see how I could know."

"Agnes, you are not Hengist."

"As near as makes no matter," said Ninian. "What is the difference?"

"They are all themselves, Mr. Middleton. It is for me to remember it."

"I am old enough to be here," said Agnes. "I understand most of the talk."

"Agnes, you are not Lavinia," said Miss Starkie, true to her idea of her duty.

"How can I be like her, if we are kept apart? I don't learn so much upstairs."

"Well, tell us what you have learnt," said Miss Starkie, as though disposing of the matter.

"They are not things that go into words."

"There, I thought so. So there is an end of it."

"And they are not things you would ever need," said Agnes, as if to herself.

"They are not, if they cannot be expressed. True and definite things for me! The others can go by the board."

"I thought you would think in that way. It is not only those things that are true."

"Agnes, I don't understand your mood."

"A mood can't be understood. I am not in one as often as the others."

"I should have thought they were always in one," said Selina.

Her grand-daughter gave a laugh.

"And how am I to get to know Mamma, if I am never with her?"

"You will know her in time," said Miss Starkie. "She does not want you always at her elbow."

"She would not say that kind of thing. I know that already about her."

"Agnes!" said Selina, sitting up and deepening her tones. "Are you going to obey Miss Starkie or are you not? It is time we knew."

"I shall have to. But it won't be for always. I can think of that."

"Agnes, you are not yourself to-day," said Miss Starkie, as if finding this unnatural thought.

"I am beginning to be. That is what it is. Not my full self yet, of course," said Agnes, following Miss Starkie, and leaving her to fill in the gap suggested.

"Which of them won?" said Egbert.

"Agnes," said Selina. "She is growing up. And that is our first victory. I suppose it is right."

"I should not have thought a victory was ever right," said Lavinia. "To judge from what I have read. But sometimes it is essentially justified."

"It is a pity the child is the father of the man," said Hugo. "Its being the other way round is quite enough."

"I would never acknowledge my early self as my father," said Egbert "I should be ashamed."

"What of yours, Lavinia?" said Selina.

"Well, there has been a certain change, Grandma. But shame is a strong word."

"It is not only the early self that causes that."

"Egbert felt it caused the most. And it may be true."

"I think a later one may cause us more."

CHAPTER VII

"So it has come," said Selina, "come at last! What might have come each day for years. He will not let me die without him. That is how I have lived. Why is it thought that death is what counts? Why is the end of life the meaning of it?"

"Ransom is returning!" said Ninian. "After so much of his life and ours! Now we have so much to forget."

"So I can say I can depart in peace," said Selina, taking the initiative upon herself.

"This is not the time to say it," said her son. "The letter will be his own. He will depend on a welcome, as if he had always wanted it.

'My dear Mother,

I am returning to you, a man of fifty-two, to see you before I die. I shall not live longer than you, possibly not so long. I have sowed too many wild oats, and am reaping what I sowed. I have also reaped substance to serve me to the end, and to serve others after me. I have taken a house near yours, there to end my days. I waited to write until I was settled in it. You know I do things to please myself. I shall come to see you at my own time. You can feel I am still your second son. You will find me altered in body, but in nothing else. No one but a mother could have a welcome for me. No one but you will have one.

Your loving son,
Ransom Middleton.'

So change is upon us. And he himself will find a change."

"I wish I had altered," said Hugo. "It will be humbling to be the same."

"It will not only be you," said Ninian. "Ransom is not different, and does not claim to be."

"Why can he be proud of his failings? Most of us have to disguise them. That may be his reason for pride. He dares to be himself."

"It might need courage. But he is what he has always been. He says it himself, and we need not doubt him. My mother is to wait in suspense until he comes. His mother too, and a woman of her age! And her age is a thing he does not forget or expect her to."

"I don't want him to be different," said Selina. "I want him as he was, as I have thought of him. Why should you all be the same? You are yourselves and must be what you are."

"If we were the same as Ransom, you would have had no sons. We accept the exaltation of the wanderer. He was lost and is found. And we are glad he is to give you what he has left, and has something left to give. But those who have not forsaken you have given more."

"My sons, you are ever with me. All that I have is yours. But Ransom has never been dead to me. His life has gone on with mine. I don't look for the young man who left me. I look for a man in middle age, as he looks for an old woman. But I can't have him die before me. When I die, I must leave him to his life. He will get strength from his mother. I can't have him back to lose him. Do you think he means what he says?"

"He would hardly say it otherwise. It would be too heartless a thing. But we will hope he is mistaken. We must wait to judge. Waiting is what he has arranged for us."

"Ah, you have never cared for him. You have never seen him as a brother. But to me you are both my sons."

"He has been the first to you. And he will be so again,

when he is with you. He will be a change for you. You are not wearied of him and his ways. But what if it was so with all of us? What if we had all left you?"

"What reason is there to imagine it? Your lives and needs were different. You have been held by your inheritance. Hugo has been glad of a home. He has not earned as Ransom has. I wonder how Ransom has done it. Well, we are soon to know."

"I doubt it. I noticed it was not revealed. I daresay it will never be."

"Well, earning is always fair. We pay for what we need. The difference is simply that people need different things. If anyone has not earned, it is because he has given nothing. You yourself look after the land and earn in your own way."

"We should not always fancy a reference to ourselves," said Hugo. "But suppose there is one?"

"What of the two elder children?" said Selina, as the voices of these were heard. "What have you given and earned there?—Come in, both of you. There is a great word to be said. Your Uncle Ransom has returned. He may be here at any time. Come in, Teresa, and wait for him with us. This is a moment for us all. My Ransom, my especial son, the one who has my name! We will welcome him together. It is not a thing for me alone. I shall know him when I see him. We shall know each other. He will not be different to me. I shall not to him."

Selina's voice broke and she groped for her handkerchief, unable to put her hand on it. Lavinia took one from the pocket of her coat, bringing something with it, that fell to the ground. She moved quickly to retrieve it, but her father forestalled her, and was handing it to her when it caught his glance. He stood with his eyes on it, looked at his daughter and back at it, and at length spoke.

"What is this, Lavinia?"

"That? Oh, I don't know. What is it?"

"It is an envelope addressed to me by Teresa. The

postmark has the date of the letter that was found in your grandmother's desk. How do you explain it?"

"Has it? What of it? I must have picked it up in her room. It was accounted for, wasn't it?"

Ninian drew from the envelope a small paper-knife belonging to Lavinia, and looked her in the eyes.

"Tell me about it, my daughter."

"What is there to tell? I must have seen the envelope, and put it in my pocket without thinking. And I suppose the knife was there. I often carry it about with me. Why should I have thought of it? If there was anything wrong about it, I should have destroyed the envelope. It means nothing."

"It means what it does. I wish you had destroyed it. Or perhaps I should not wish it. It is right that the truth should emerge. Tell me the whole."

"You tell it to me. You know more of it than I do. The matter means nothing to me. It is to you; it seems to mean something. Do you know about it?"

"Lavinia, this is no good. The truth is thrust on us. We are helpless before it. Tell it to us yourself."

"You have told it, my son," said Selina. "We do not need it again."

"He is implying something," said Lavinia, turning between them as if bewildered. "I can only guess what it is. The letter was in your desk, Grandma. And the envelope must have fallen on the floor. And I suppose I picked it up. It is what anyone would do. Such things do not leave a memory."

"Why did you put the letter in the desk, my child? I have never quite understood. Why did you not destroy it?"

"Do we destroy other people's letters? I thought they were sacrosanct. If I came on this one, and put it in the desk for you to read, it was a natural thing to do. And an easy thing to forget. I should not have known what was in it. We do not read people's letters either."

95

"The paper-knife tells its tale," said Ninian. "There is no need to make another."

"You thought I was going to die?" said Selina, her eyes still on her grand-daughter.

"We were all afraid of it, Grandma. But that does not bear on the matter."

"Then the letter would have been found after my death, and the guilt assigned to me? And to my conscious self that time."

"I don't know anything about the letter. Except that Father read it to us."

"A service you did not need," said Ninian. "Have you known all the time, Mother?"

"I could not know. I have thought it. I knew it was not any self of mine. And who could it have been? Who had an end to serve? Who—it is best to say it at once—sorted the letters when they came? Who was distraught and not in command of herself?"

"Then you were shielding Lavinia?"

"Well, I had no proof. And an unconscious self is a useful shield. There is no question of blame."

"What have you to say, my daughter?"

"Nothing," said Lavinia, in a sudden, hard tone, as if casting off a guise. "I thought it a service to you to hide the letter, a service to us all. Yes, and the greatest to myself. It would have saved us from wrong and wretchedness, as I saw the matter then."

"Why did you not destroy it, as your grandmother said?"

"It might have transpired that Teresa had sent it," said Lavinia, in an almost exasperated tone, as if this should be clear.

"But should we have suspected you? You of all people? You know we should not."

"There would have been discussion and question. And the letters went through my hands, as Grandma has also said."

96

"You thought we should find the letter in the end?"

"You would have gone through Grandma's papers," said Lavinia, with an open sigh.

"That is most of it," said Selina. "And the rest I know. It was too much to destroy the letter. The wrong of it would have been too great. Poor child!"

"We must try to see her in that way," said Ninian. "It is not as she has seen herself."

"And not as you have seen her," said Teresa. "That must be said. It may be at the root of everything."

"The guilt is not mine. I had my own right to happiness. If I was making too large a part of hers, it was time I ceased. It was time indeed. Perhaps it was too late. Perhaps I am partly to blame. It would help me to feel I was."

"So I have been the cause of it all."

"Not you yourself," said Lavinia. "Anyone in your place."

"You took a great risk. Few of us would have dared to take it. So much depends on our courage."

"I am grieved to the heart," said Ninian.

A low voice came from the door, where Miss Starkie stood with the children.

"Would you like to come upstairs, Lavinia?"

"No, thank you. Nothing would be gained."

"You share my grief, Miss Starkie," said Ninian. "It is especially yours and mine."

"I can hardly believe it, Mr. Middleton. I feel it cannot be true."

"We all felt in that way. It was forced upon us. Lavinia herself has said it now."

"I don't understand about it," said Leah, in an undertone.

"I do," said Hengist, half-smiling. "I will tell you upstairs."

"You will not," said Miss Starkie, in an unfamiliar tone. "You will neither of you utter a word of it, now or ever. It is a thing you will not dare to do."

97

"I haven't said a word," said Agnes. "I knew it was that kind of thing."

"We are not always with her," said Hengist, glancing at Miss Starkie.

"I trust you," said the latter, looking at him. "You must be worthy of trust."

"Are you worthy?" said Leah in a whisper.

"No. And it is no good to try to be, when you are not."

"Not even Lavinia seems to be," said Leah, her tone awed.

"I must speak at last," said Hugo to Egbert. "Have we to believe it?"

"Yes. The idea had occurred to me. But I thought it could not be."

"It can't. Not as it seems. It was fate, her father, anything. She is a pawn in the game."

"Lavinia could not be a pawn. She laid her plan. She was serving the common cause."

"Her own first of all. That was rare and resolute in her. It is so unusual to serve ourselves. All the talk is of serving others. It draws me closer to her. Teresa saw something of the truth. Would you have dared to do it?"

"No, or perhaps I might have. As I say, the thought had struck me. So I must have felt it possible. Is it a protection to have no courage?"

"Should you not say a word to the person who showed it?"

"Yes, I have planned the word. It is what I have been doing. I hope it will not fail."

Egbert moved to his sister.

"Lavinia, I have seen you as the heroine of a drama. And you have emerged as the opposite. But it is the latter who carries our sympathy. Think of the examples in books, the very best ones."

"Well, is this a case in life?" said Lavinia, holding her eyes from him, and unconscious of her clenched hands. "I hardly think it will be. But it is a clever word."

"It is an honest one. It comes from my heart. And I could not have faced the danger. I should simply have been afraid. What a waste it has been!"

"I forgot that one thing we are known to forget. Or are found to have forgotten, when it has betrayed us. In my case the envelope with the paper-knife. Perhaps it shows I am not hardened."

"You have needed to be. Dire things have come upon you."

"I have simply not realised them. I don't realise what is on me now. You are remembering things I said. I can see they are coming back to you. I shall never be trusted again. I shall live under a cloud. But perhaps no one is trusted much. Or I can try to think so."

"Grandma emerges as a great figure. I feel I have not known her."

"And have not known me. I suppose she has known us all. I half-fancied she suspected. Or I think now that I did. But I somehow felt I was safe with her. I almost felt I had her sympathy. Unless I imagine that too."

"I like the wisdom after the event," said Hugo. "It tends to be real wisdom. The other has so often to be disowned."

"How I envy you both!" said Lavinia. "For your ease both now and for the future."

"If I inspired envy, it would be for a negative reason."

"I am thinking of Father," said Egbert. "And so are both of you. I wonder what he really feels."

"He has not disguised it," said Lavinia. "You can be in no doubt."

"It was a moment of shock. He can hardly be judged by it."

"Well, things are comparative. I had not thought of the moments for him. It was an unusual one for you all."

"What was it for Miss Starkie?" said Hugo. "Somehow we are not sure."

"That is still before me. Grandma was easy; Father was

obvious; you are yourselves. And all of you are over. I don't know what she will be."

"And I am myself," said Teresa's voice. "I see no reason to be different. You minded my coming as much as this?"

"I could not face the loss of my father. It seemed to break up my world. You remember I did not know you. You will not want to know me, now that you do."

"As much as ever. Even more than I did. We all have it in us to do those things. There have been times when I might have done them, if I had dared. But you had no fear?"

"I had a greater one. And it was also as Grandma said. It need not be said again. She knows the confusion in us. She knows too much ever to be really surprised. Well, you must all be learning."

"I should always be surprised," said Hugo. "I am so surprised by this, that I don't believe in it. It has no truth. It was the result of the stress of things. You were forced out of yourself."

"Or into myself. I meant the wrong to be hidden. And in that case we might all become ourselves. I try to think Teresa is right."

"Would you say it to Father, Teresa?" said Egbert. "Think of him and think of Lavinia."

"Not of us both together," said his sister. "There is no reason to give rein to thought. And now he and I will be apart. Well, you may say I have brought it all on myself."

"We should not dream of it," said Hugo. "And it would not be true. You did all you could to escape it."

"With little success. This will follow me through my life."

"It must, my daughter," said Ninian's voice. "And in a way it should be a protection to you. May it be."

"She does not need one," said Teresa. "It was her feeling for you that caused it. It will hardly cause it again. But it should not be forgotten. Anyhow by you."

"It is not forgotten by me. It has been my support.

My sense of it has enabled me to shoulder some of the blame. And so to lessen hers."

"I wonder you have not more value for such a feeling. None of your other children has it."

"Is this the moment for me to value it?" said Ninian, speaking sadly. "Or for you to wish me to? What might it have done for us?"

"All feeling leads to blindness on other scores. She forgot your claims as you forgot hers. You forget them now."

"Is it the time to remember them?" said Ninian, in the same tone. "We see what her sense of them led to."

"Or what forgetting them did."

"Come to me, Lavinia," said her grandmother. "We are people apart. We may be of help to each other."

"There is none for me, Grandma. I feel I am hardly alive. I am afraid to hear or feel. I hardly know if I do. Or if I ever shall again. I suppose I shall not dare to."

"This first onset will pass. And each one will be less. And in the end they will cease."

"What do you feel yourself? About the sacrifice I made of you? Tell me. I shall hardly hear. I shall feel nothing."

"The main wrong led to lesser ones. Such a thing goes beyond itself. When we break our bonds, we release the whole of us. And only part should be free, the part we present as the whole."

"If that is wisdom, it is wasted. I can't listen to words. I must go away from here. I can't stay in my home. And I have no money, I have never thought of it or needed it. I can't be seen as I shall be now. It has been so different. What am I to do?"

"What people do, who have been found out. Wait for the trouble to subside. Suffer it when it arises. Fight it, if it is too much. There is nothing else for you. And the worst is behind. You have little more to dread."

"Father will never be behind. And there is Miss Starkie before me."

"Oh, Miss Starkie," said Selina.

"She has exalted me from the first. She had come almost to look up to me."

"Well, that will end. And it is better that it should. It must appear that it is not your place. And you do not depend on her."

"She does on me. This will alter her life in the house."

"It need not affect yours. Do not give too much of yourself. You will meet with no return."

"No, I have found it. Father had no thought of making any. I have gained Teresa against his will. She has been better to me than anyone but you. She has not even made light of it, as Uncle and Egbert have."

"You wanted it taken as it was? It was what they tried to avoid."

"Whatever I had done, I was in a hopeless plight."

"And you wanted it greater, pushed to its limit? I know what you mean. It would have meant the end. But it would have been too much."

"We are supposed to be better for our stumbles. I am not."

"We are wiser. Not better. We are what we are."

"It is true of me. What do you think of it, Grandma?"

"I am old. I have seen and heard. I know that things are done. Temptation is too much for us. We are not always unwilling for it to be."

"All I did was to put a letter in your desk, instead of giving it to Father."

"Yes, that was all," said Selina.

"Many people have done worse things."

"Than harming a father's life? Well, some are worse."

"I felt he would not be happy with Teresa."

"Yes. It was he who felt he would."

"And I don't think he is very happy."

"He is having what he can. It is she who is looking aside."

"Do you mean I am harming his life in another way?"

"You did not succeed in the first. You can hardly help the second. And he has harmed yours. More than he needed for his ends."

"You have not a high opinion of people, Grandma."

"Why should I have? What of the examples before me?"

"You are shocked by what I have done."

"I am shocked that you should do it. That is not speaking against you."

"Should we dare to say it, Uncle?" said Egbert, as they overheard.

"I don't know. And it does not matter. The trouble is that it was Lavinia. And that her trouble was so great. A dreadful question arises. Who will sort the letters now?"

"How true it is that small things can be the worst! One of us had better do it and say nothing."

"It would be best for Lavinia to go on doing it. As if nothing had happened."

"Unless Father behaves as if something has."

"What are you discussing?" said Ninian.

"Oh, nothing, Father."

"Nothing, of course. In other words our trouble. But what aspect of it?"

"Only a minor one, Father."

"Of course. The main one is dealt with. And it presents no question."

"This is not worth mentioning," said Hugo.

"Then why did you find it so?"

"Pray do not talk like the head of the family, Ninian. Suppose someone should hear you!"

"I do what I must in the place. I should know the temper of the house. What is the minor point you speak of?"

"It was really a question."

"Yes?" said Ninian.

"Well, answer it, if you can. Who is to sort the letters now?"

There was a pause.

"I will sort them myself."

"Would it not be better for Egbert or me to do it?"

"For what reason?"

"It would call less attention to the change."

"There will be no question. I am the head of the house, as we have said."

"Well, you have," said Hugo. "Who will tell Lavinia? If you say you will do that yourself, I will forestall you."

"I am glad for you to do it. It will be at less cost to us all," said Ninian, as he turned away. "Tell her also that I shall not mention it."

"So Father is more sensitive than we are," said Egbert.

"Yes. He felt he had to tell us. And we did not know."

"And he is afraid of Lavinia. That is a happy thing. I am afraid of her, and so are you. And suppose he was the only one who was not!"

"I am afraid of what she feels. It must be on the scale of herself. Will you tell her about the letters? If her father can shrink from it, so can I."

Egbert turned to his sister.

"Lavinia, you have asked yourself a question. I am able to answer it."

"I have asked myself so many. Tell me just the answer."

"Father is to sort the letters in future."

"Oh! I had forgotten. Yes, I suppose he is. And I think it falls to him. But what will the servants say?"

"I had not thought of that. We never think of everything. If we did, you would have destroyed that envelope."

"It is supposed to be good for us to be found out. I have so far felt no benefit."

"The benefit is moral. And so better for other people than for us."

"Did Father tell you he would sort the letters?"

"The subject came up. And he said he would do it.

And he will not speak of it to you. I hope he is afraid."

"We can hardly be at ease about the matter. I am glad to be spared. The moment could only be itself. What hours they have been! I have hardly been alive to them. But something has gone deep and will follow me. And there are things to come."

"Surely there is nothing more."

"The daily facing of Father. The being less at ease with you and Grandma; yes, even with you. Uncle is the exception. I don't know why."

"I believe I do," said Hugo. "You feel I might have done what you have."

"Would you have dared?" said Lavinia.

"No wonder you are at ease with me. We always are with people we look down on."

"She has to be revenged on people," said Egbert. "They appear to be better than she is. And she does not believe they are. No one could forgive them."

Ninian came up to his daughter.

"Lavinia, the hour is behind us. It has been a dark one for us both. For me there is a weight of sorrow, and for you the heavier weight of your own. But nothing need prevent our going forward, as nothing can prevent our looking back. This is my last word of it. If part of the blame is mine, that is my atonement."

He laid his hand on her shoulder and moved away, signing to his wife to follow. She remained where she was, and spoke to him across the distance.

"There have been too many words. You should know the time to forget. There are different kinds of wrong. The people sinned against are not always the best."

"They are not," said a sudden, deep voice. "They might be doing better now. It is a happy chance that I am here."

CHAPTER VIII

"Ransom!" said Selina. "Ransom, my son! You are with your mother. You are in your home. Other things are nothing. My life is not at its end. The best of it is to come."

There appeared a large, dark man, who would have borne a likeness to Selina, but for a heaviness that cumbered his features and his frame, and somehow told of failing health. He had stood by the door with Miss Starkie, seeking enlightenment as he needed it. The former had dismissed her pupils, and herself retained her place. He stood with his arm about his mother and spoke to anyone who heard him.

"The girl can come with me. My house is near. Home is not the place at such a time. It has no help for the young who have stumbled by the way. I can recognise the real wrong-doer. A wanderer has his use. Miss Starkie will see she is ready. We shall be going in an hour."

Lavinia obeyed Miss Starkie's sign and followed her. She did not question the decision. It spelt escape.

"I have come back to have my way. I am the man I was. And no one will care what I do. In outstaying my welcome I have outstayed everything else. But I have come to be near my home, and to leave what I have to support it. Money comes to the just and unjust. It has come in a measure to me. I have resisted temptation and yielded to it. There is not much in many lives. I can rescue the niece who has met it. She will be with me and order my house. And at the same time I serve myself. Yes, your thought is true and clear. And now I will be with my mother. She and I have the shortest future, and have shared the least of the past."

"You know I have married a wife," said Ninian. "You will be a friend to her?"

"Yes, I know. And I have seen and heard. And I am her friend."

Ransom sat down by Selina, and she heard him and understood. Her son had returned to her to leave her. He had numbered his days.

Ninian waited for a time and then came up to them.

"Ransom, we rejoice that you are with us. We wish we could rejoice more. It is your health that brings you to us? You would not be here, if you were well?"

"It is true. I bring my doomed self to those who have not seen my prime. I return to my mother less as a joy than a grief. But from you I should have a welcome. Her loss will be your gain. My death will ensure your future. It is you who will have what is mine. The place that calls for it is yours."

"The welcome is from all of us," said Ninian, passing over the last words. "And indeed you have it. And you must not give up hope."

"I have done what I could, asked and followed what I could. My heart has had its day. I have worked it hard. I have lived hard myself. It has to fail in its time. But here is something I can do first."

"I am dazzled by you, Ransom," said Hugo. "I don't mean you put me in the shade, as I no longer notice it. I look out on a light. You bring out the poet in me. I know there is one in you."

"Have you always been here?" said Ransom.

"That is a question hard to forgive. But I am a person who must forgive it. Yes. Where else should I have been?"

"What have you been doing all these years?"

"No one could forgive that. And even I cannot answer it."

"There can be no answer. I have none myself. You compare well enough with me."

"No, there is wonder in returning. And after we had

given up hope. That adds to your value, though it hardly seems it should. And what wonder is there in always being here? The kind you showed."

"A better kind, my boy,"said Selina. "A kind we feel without knowing it."

"But I wish you knew it. You know you feel the other kind."

"Now I am in the shade," said Ransom. "We may be two dimmed figures. But we have the third."

"Now listen to me," said Miss Starkie's voice. "You are not here to attract attention. I have brought you to greet your uncle. You will just say good-night and go."

"That is not greeting him," said Hengist.

"Well, it hardly is," said Ransom, with his eyes on them. "I will accept a little more. How are you both?"

"We are quite well, thank you," said Leah.

"I am glad to hear it. I cannot say the same."

"You look quite well," said Hengist.

"Perhaps he is ashamed of it," said Leah. "Cook and Nurse would be."

"How do you do, Uncle?" said Agnes. "I think you are like Grandma."

"Do you see that for yourself?" said Ransom, looking at her.

"She has heard people say it," said Hengist.

"Do you think I am like her?" said his uncle.

"No, you are too—you are not as thin as she is."

"Well, I am a very sick man."

"That would make him thin," said Leah.

"Hush; it does not always," said Miss Starkie. "Now that is enough. Say good-night and come away."

The children kissed Selina and their father, smiled at Teresa and went to the door.

"Have you forgotten me already?" said Ransom.

"We don't go round to everyone," said Leah. "We didn't go to Uncle Hugo, and we can't have forgotten him."

"You could have said good-night on the first day," said Miss Starkie, in a tone without hope. "You know I brought you down on purpose."

"Why are you staying so late?" said Hengist, in one without gratitude.

"I have been helping Lavinia. She is going to stay with your uncle."

"So he doesn't mind what she has done," said Leah.

"You will not speak of it," said Miss Starkie.

"We don't mind about it either," said Hengist. "So we shouldn't say anything that mattered."

"You will say nothing at all," said Miss Starkie, as she closed the door.

"It is late for me to know them," said Ransom to his brother. "And they will not have time to know me. I shall not be missed."

"Which do you take to the most?"

"The small, dark girl of those. Most of all to the girl who will be mine. I saw and heard before you did."

"You could hardly have understood."

"I had Miss Starkie at my elbow. There you have chosen well. I was not long in the dark."

"She does make her impression on people," said Selina.

"Lavinia needs a change," said Ninian. "She can be with you for a time."

"She has no choice. Where else is she to be?"

"She could stay in her home. What if you had not returned?"

"We will shun the thought, as she does."

"What shall we do without her?" said Egbert.

"You can stand on your own feet," said his father.

"Neither of us does so. We depend on each other."

"Come to see her when you like," said Ransom.

"Thank you, Uncle, I will."

"I will not come often at first," said Ninian.

"No, you must earn your welcome."

"I am Lavinia's father."

"So you are learning it. Come when you have done so."

"You talk as if I were a stern father. Lavinia has not been dealt with hardly. She has to learn right from wrong. Indeed she knows it."

"There are many kinds of wrong, as has been said."

"If Lavinia were your child, you would feel as I do."

"We cannot be sure. I hope I should feel as I do now."

"Unmarried people's children are always the best managed."

"If that is true, take a lesson from one."

"I may come with Egbert to see Lavinia?" said Hugo.

"Yes, as often as you please."

"And I too?" said Teresa.

"Yes, yes, as often."

"I don't see much good in her leaving home, if she is to be followed by everyone," said Ninian.

"Not by everyone," said Ransom. "And not to her home."

"Ransom, I am glad from my heart to welcome you. And grieved to my heart by the news of your health. I hope my girl will be a comfort to you. I may be allowed to say that."

"I hope so too. I have thought of it. I shall serve myself."

"You will not take a light view of the trouble? It is the last thing for her at this time."

"I take none. At this time, as you say. She has her own knowledge of it."

"Well, I can do nothing," said Ninian.

"No, you have done what you could. We say that no one can do more. And that may be fortunate, considering the conditions under which it is usually said."

"You talk in a strange way. Lavinia has been my dearest child."

"Has been? What is she? What is she to be? You needed a companion and used her as one. And threw her away when you chose another. It had to lead to something, and it led to this. It means nothing."

"Did Miss Starkie tell you all this?"

"She answered my questions. She did not know what she told me. She is used to teaching with her mind astray."

"The letters have come, ma'am," said Ainger at the door, his eyes wavering from Selina to Teresa in an uncertainty he had not resolved. "Will Miss Lavinia sort them?"

"She is going to stay with Mr. Ransom," said Ninian. "I will sort them for her. And in future I will do it myself."

"What is behind it, Cook?" said Ainger in the hall. "There is something beyond even me."

"Well, is your sphere so wide? And complacence occurs as we go downwards."

"Then you can look for it in me," said another voice. "And expect to find it."

"I do not look for anything in you, James. The idea not having struck me. And is the hall your place?—And when I speak, I await reply."

"You didn't speak to me."

"Oh, there is this trouble with the name, Cook," said Ainger, idly. "He is one thing to himself and another to everyone else."

"I am myself and no other person," said James, with a heat the words hardly seemed to warrant.

"And is it so much to be?" said Cook. "That you claim it in the face of everything? The self you refer to is known as James, to those who are aware of it."

"I am myself and not the last boy."

"It is a good thing you are not both. But whichever you are, you hear who speaks," said Ainger, perhaps hardly avoiding the resented confusion.

"Yes," said James, more faintly, glancing at Cook.

"Yes—?"

"Yes, sir," said James, as he disappeared.

"Not a penny of mine for his thoughts," said Ainger. "They are not worth it."

"They are hardly my concern, his actions happening to suffice."

"But I am glad I am not under anyone."

"We are all under Someone, Ainger. I am myself," said Cook, in full humility.

"Are you indeed? Is it a piece of news? You would hardly be the Someone, I suppose?"

"I should not," said Cook, gravely. "You are right to suppose it. It not being a matter for doubt."

"I sometimes wonder how much doubt you have of it."

"I am silent, Ainger, the words not calling for reply."

The speakers moved aside, as Lavinia came downstairs, and Selina and her sons and grandson entered the hall. Ninian's glance went to his daughter's coat, swept over the pocket and withdrew. Hugo and Egbert followed it and dropped their eyes.

"Good-bye, my child," said Selina. "Be careful of yourself and my son. I am glad to feel you are with him."

"Good-bye, my daughter," said Ninian, stooping to her gravely and saying no more.

"I will not say good-bye," said Teresa. "I shall see you too soon."

"Anyone can see her, who wants to do that," said Ransom.

The uncle and niece went together from the house, seeming in their different ways to lean on each other. Ninian waited for the carriage to start, and turned away. Selina sat down in the hall and sank into tears.

"What is it, Mother?" said her son.

"So you need to ask? You cannot need to know."

"It is Ransom. But we hope for the best. Anyhow you have seen him again."

"When I might have had him always! How little I have had! How little!"

Ninian led her away and the others followed them.

"If anything else happens," said Egbert, "I shall not

be conscious of it. I can't be alive to any more. But I hardly think anything can. It has all done so."

"We must take our courage in both hands. If we take it in one, perhaps we cannot use it. There are still things to come. Ransom will die; Lavinia will return; your father will sort the letters. There will only be one change from the past, but what a change!"

Selina sat down on a lower chair than usual, looking smaller than usual herself. She spoke as if continuing her words.

"I had rather he was well and away from me, than with me and near to his death. He is to lose everything. Others will have what is his. They will have what he has worked for. And they would rather have it than him. Their thought is on themselves."

"It is on their home and mine, as his has been," said Ninian. "It is his wish that we should have it, and our descendants after us. Not to welcome it would show ingratitude, and be unworthy of us and him."

"Yes, you may be grateful. You must be. You will have everything and he will have nothing. And I shall not have my son."

"You have hardly had him for many years," said Hugo.

"As much as I have had you. I have looked for his letters and thought of him. And it is everything to hope."

"And you have valued him for his absence," said Ninian. "You have imagined him more than himself. That is why his presence has failed you."

Selina turned away and sank into herself and silence.

"So your future is safe, Ninian," said Hugo. "Ransom is your benefactor, and you are humbled before him. But your mother would humble you too far."

"She may exalt him as much as she pleases," said Ninian, in a rising tone. "A great burden is lifted off me, a threat from the lands of my fathers. I have lived alone with the anxiety. I will share the relief. As I realise it, I grudge him nothing. I grudge myself what I shall have, that should be his. I grudge myself my very gratitude. But it comes from my heart. I hope I shall be able to show it."

"I am sure you will. You seem to have a gift for it. And it is a rare one."

"How seldom people really rejoice!" said Egbert. "There is usually an alloy."

"There is one here," said Ninian gravely. "It is nearer to me than to you. But my brother knows we would help it, if we could; that we will, if we can. And he will see the good that is to come. I will not disguise my debt."

"Debts do meet another fate. But will he be content with the reward?"

"He will not deem it nothing. It is what he chose of what could be his."

"He may feel that nothing can be his. Most people would in his place."

"You are not my friend, my boy," said Ninian, looking at him. "But it is your future in my mind as much as my own. Yours and your children's children's. I must not see you as a friend, but I am your father."

There was a pause.

"I can only wish I could bear this moment for you, Egbert," said Hugo.

"Yes, I take less thought for my descendants than their great-grandfather does."

"Yes, turn it off easily," said Ninian. "It is the thing to do. But I meant what I said."

"That is why it was so awkward," said Hugo. "It sounded as if you did."

"We cannot be silent beyond a point. There could be no reason."

"Well, you were not. But we can be up to a point."

"You might both be boys," said Ninian. "Your every word suggests it."

"I see it is my place. And Ransom is doing nothing about it."

"Your home will be safe as well as mine. My house is

yours. But we are never grateful for a thing, when someone else has more of it."

"What a day it has been!" said Hugo. "There is
material for an epic. The fall of Lavinia; the return of
Ransom; the uplift of Ninian; the tragedy of Ransom; the
escape of Lavinia; the lament of Selina. I hope there will
be no more."

"And the lament of Egbert," said Ninian, gently,
looking at his son. "It has not been spoken, but it has
not been unheard. My boy, I know what the day has been
for you. I know how you felt to your sister."

"As I now feel to her, Father. She has not failed me."

"I wish I could feel the same and say it."

"I wish you had said it. She encountered forces too
strong for her. And you know what they were."

Selina passed with a faltering tread, conscious of it,
if not causing it. And as it died away another followed.

"It is only me, Mr. Middleton. Only I, I should say. I
am late in leaving the scene of my efforts to-day."

"That is what it has been, I fear. It is good of you to
help us."

"It is good to be needed. That should be enough."

"Suppose I were in your place!" said Hugo. "And
people needed me!"

"Ah, you have your word, Mr. Hugo. But you are there
in case of need. And you know what is said of those who
only stand and wait."

"I do. And I feel I may suggest it. I suppose our fears
about ourselves are always well founded."

"Ah, they are great words, Mr. Hugo," said Miss
Starkie, yielding to the didactic spirit, as she went to
the door. "And they would be, even if we did not know
from whom they came."

"And that is not true of all great words. How clever and
disillusioned you are! I must remember to say it."

"Stay for a moment, Miss Starkie," said Ninian. "We
have our word to say. Our reluctance to say it shows it

must be said. We make our judgement in order to forget it. It must be what it is."

"Yes, we must not evade it, Mr. Middleton. It is unworthy to shrink from the truth. If we faltered in our guidance, it is we who have failed. It is ourselves whom we judge."

There was a pause.

"Yes, I feel it indeed. The words might be mine," said Ninian, accompanying her to the hall. "It is a thing in which we must be at one."

"So your father had to make a false claim," said Hugo. "It seemed to come easily to him. How much practice has he had? Miss Starkie judged him by herself. His mind is a sealed book to her."

"I wish it was to me. Why isn't it, when so many minds are?"

"I hardly think Miss Starkie's is. Anyhow she has unsealed it."

"I am given both a better and a worse character than I deserve," said Ninian, returning in a manner at once absent and constrained. "I am neither so generous in shouldering blame nor guilty of so much."

"Why could you not say so?" said Hugo.

Ninian just raised his brows.

"People used to instructing cannot accept instruction. It would have been to waste words. But it is no tribute to anyone to shift the just blame."

"But it lessens what does not take the form of tribute."

Ninian moved his brows again and turned to find Teresa at his side.

"What does my wife think about it?"

"I liked what Miss Starkie said. Even if it is not the whole truth."

"Ah, that would lead us into perilous ways. There would be danger for my poor Lavinia."

"Not of a kind that mattered. Not compared to her losing her feeling for her father."

"Oh, I don't think that danger is very great," said Ninian, with easy candour. "It was in that feeling that the danger lay."

"You don't take your daughter as seriously as you took her trouble."

"I am advised by Miss Starkie that she is not responsible. I am not allowed to take her as I would choose. But perhaps I may be persuaded. I should naturally like to be."

"I can't understand why she felt so much for you."

"Come, come, who should understand it but you? And why the past tense? Has she lost the feeling? Oh, no, I don't think so. And all this is to be forgotten. And the feeling will return as we both forget."

"I don't follow this lighter treatment of a thing you took with such solemnity."

"The solemnity was disapproved. And I don't wonder, if that was the word. It was not, as you know. My trouble was real and remains so."

"It seems to be less," said his wife.

"Well, we do not cling to a sense of someone's sin. We let it fade in its day. We will leave it and have an hour with my mother. Other things have a claim."

"What things?" said Hugo, as the door closed. "Or rather what thing? Are you too sensitive to frame the thought?"

"I must be, because I dismissed it. Are you going to put it into words?"

"It is the promise of Ransom's money. Everything pales beside it. And it is also a promise for you, and so for Lavinia."

"For the distant future. It does nothing for her youth or mine. Nothing for her after my uncle's death. What does she feel about living with him?"

"It is the alternative to being here, and being with her father. And to being with you and me. We did our best. And no one can do more. But that is a great pity."

"If only we could identify ourselves with what she did!"

"Yes, we failed her there. And it was not a failure that was greater than success. And she did not think so."

"What hours those have been! I shall welcome an ordinary day."

"I shall not. I should have to make a habit of it. It is a pity so much has happened on one. It could have gone much further."

"If it had not been for this, Uncle Ransom would have lived alone. That may have influenced him."

"Yes, I saw him being influenced."

"You see so much," said Egbert.

"Yes, it has been my life work. And I can feel I have done it well."

"Will Uncle Ransom leave anything to you?"

"I have asked myself that, as I could not ask him. No one thinks of my wanting anything. I never speak of it, as it is humbling to have needs that are not fulfilled. And people would wonder what I should do with money, if I had it. And I have had no chance to learn."

"To learn what?" said Ninian, returning to the room.

"What to do with money. It is a thing you know."

"I know it well. Its uses are indeed defined. There is none over."

"I don't dare to voice my thought."

"No, do not voice it," said Ninian, in a grave tone. "It is not mine. Ransom is my younger brother. It is his right to outlive me. I hope he will. If not, the disposal of what is his, is a question for him alone."

"He has answered it, Father," said Egbert.

"He can give it any other answer. If he does, we shall see it as the right one."

"I admire nobility," said Hugo. "But it is a pity for it to be wasted. You can accept the truth."

"I cannot, for the reasons I have given. It is not the truth to me."

"I suppose he might leave everything to Lavinia," said Egbert, lightly.

"I suppose nothing."

"Or divide it between all of us."

"I suppose nothing," said his father.

"What do you feel about Lavinia's being with him?" said Hugo.

"A young girl with an ageing man in uncertain health? It is late to ask me what I feel. What good would it be to say?"

"He is not as old as we are. And our age does not matter any longer. It will soon be said that we get younger with every day."

"It will not be said of Ransom," said Ninian, still gravely.

"He is fortunate to have Lavinia," said Egbert. "And he showed that he thought so."

"Yes, the help is not only for her. May they both have it. I wish it from my heart. Now I must return to your grandmother. I came to fetch something for her. Other people can need help."

"Why cannot we like people in lofty moods?" said Hugo. "I suppose it is their being so unnatural to them. It produces discomfort."

"And they like themselves so much," said Egbert. "Father is ennobling himself enough to balance his dealings with Lavinia. Or can he really be what he suggests? People's views of themselves may not be always wrong."

"It is when they express it. Or why should they need to? They must know there is no evidence for it."

"Would you dare to express yours?"

"Well, I should have to ennoble myself," said Hugo.

CHAPTER IX

"A GOOD HOME, a good girl, good people in the house," said Ransom, leaning back in his doorway. "A free past and a short future. It is the last that brings the balance down."

"You feel no better, Uncle?"

"Feebler each day. It will go on and bring the end."

"The end of what I have," said Lavinia.

"Another beginning. I will see that it is. My own end is eased for me. One besides my mother will regret me. It is more than I looked for. I find it much."

"What should I have done without you?"

"We should both have been poorly placed. We have helped each other. And I have never had return before. I shall die, knowing what it is. If I recovered, would you live with me or go back to your father?"

"Live with you, Uncle. And see my father at times."

"Ah, the forces work. Nothing lives only on itself. Anything can die. And your family take no risk with you. They are on their way."

Hugo and Egbert and Teresa approached, and Ransom leaned back with his eyes on them.

"Good-day. I am glad to see you. And I can offer you the person you are glad to see."

"Your father sends his love to you, Lavinia," said Teresa. "And we can see he hopes to have yours."

"No, he has had enough of my love. I will not offer any more."

"He has begun to talk of you," said Egbert. "Your desertion has added to your value."

"On that basis mine should be high," said Ransom.

"But I hardly found it was. What are you looking at, Hugo?"

"At your house and all there is about you. A wanderer returned with provision for his needs! The situation is hardly recognised."

"It is what gives me a foothold. I should not have had one."

"You would have lived in Ninian's house," said Teresa. "That would have been your home."

"And something only a home can be. But it is a kind word."

"How did you make your money, Ransom?" said Hugo.

"Not in any way that would be useful to you."

"No way would be. So you can admit the truth."

"It was in ways accepted in their time and place."

"So you know life," said Egbert. "How strange that seems in Father's brother!"

"You have your own knowledge of it. And one I hardly feel strange in his son."

"Did you find Ninian changed?" said Hugo.

"Hardly. He is not subject to change."

"He has had the chance to be himself."

"We know he was independent of it."

"I can't imagine him in a secondary place."

"It is no good to have unnatural thoughts," said Ransom.

"Suppose he had been in mine?"

"It is the place that would have been different."

"And I have accepted it as it is?"

"You were not offered it as anything else."

"Are you a man of the world, Uncle?" said Egbert. "It is the first time I have met one."

"Only a man of the whole world. The other stays in his place."

"Then perhaps I am the other," said Hugo.

"Perhaps you are," said Ransom.

"He would be a narrower being," said Egbert.

"On the surface," said Ransom. "He is deeper and more complete."

"Then you do wish you were one?"

"I have wished I was equal to it."

"Then does Father go deep?"

"Well, he goes to his depths."

"I think that is true, Uncle," said Lavinia.

"He has shown concern about me and my end. That gives his measure. Or gives it to me."

"He feels you will live on in him," said Hugo. "I heard him say so."

"As a substitute for living yourself," said Lavinia. "It is not a good one. But there is not a better."

"Father wishes there was," said Egbert. "I am bound to say it."

"You must do justice to yourself," said Ransom. "It is a pity when it involves doing it to someone else."

"Joy for yourself is not gratitude," said Hugo.

"It is what gives rise to it," said Lavinia. "I don't think there is ever any other reason."

"Then no wonder we dislike gratitude," said Ransom. "Joy for yourself indeed!"

"Do we often meet it?" said Egbert. "We keep what is ours, until we die."

"Well, that is something. It is not so much joy for themselves. Suppose people had any more of it!"

"I am to have it, Egbert. To have my own home, where you can be with me. And where Uncle Hugo can come."

"You would have to support us both. Father would not help me."

"Ask him," said Ransom. "He is coming."

"Without permission, Uncle? I thought he was to wait for it?"

"It is not a thing he recognises. He has had his own."

"Well, is there a welcome for me?" said Ninian. "My wife and son and brothers are here. The family may as well be complete."

"You have left my mother," said Ransom.

"She has sent me for news of you. You will let me take it? And whether you want to see me or not, I am glad to see you."

"These are generous words. Do they spring from a generous heart? We were asking a question that may tell us. Would you allow this son enough money to live with his sister? When you have more of it yourself."

"No, of course I would not. They have their home, and no reason to leave it. They are only two of my five children. I have to consider them as a whole. It is what I owe to them. To do as you say would be to evade the debt."

"We were not talking quite like that, Father," said Egbert.

"I hope you were not. I would rather not think it of you."

"Are these words generous or not?" said Ransom. "I am not quite sure."

"Yours were hardly true. Is it a better thing for them to be?"

"Send your family into the garden, Ninian. And come yourself with me. We will have a word together. We shall not have many more."

"I shall like to have one, Ransom. It is long since we did so. Indeed I came with a hope of it."

Ransom led the way into the house, and sat down with his eyes on his brother.

"Will you do something for me?"

"Anything. I need not say it. I would rather it was much than little."

"It is not a great thing. I have lived over fifty years. I do not ask much of people. If you go into the other room, you will find two documents in the chest. Will you put the earlier one on the fire, and turn the key on the other? I am able for nothing myself. The dates will strike your eye. You need not read beyond them."

"I should not," said Ninian, smiling. "They are nothing

123

to do with me. Of course I will do it, Ransom. It will be a matter of a moment. But will you not come and see it done?"

"No, my sight is failing; my strength is gone. I use neither more than I must. You can do me the small service. I am not so enfeebled that my words do not count. Here is the key of the chest. I shall not go to it again."

Ninian took it and left the room, and Ransom sat with his eyes on his watch, finding that they served him.

"Too simple," he said to himself. "Too simple to hold any reason. But people who have power respond simply. They know no minds but their own."

"Thank you," he said, when Ninian returned. "Now it is done and can be forgotten."

"Yes, put such things from your thoughts. They are not in anyone else's. And there may be time for many changes."

"What things?" said Ransom easily. "Changes in what?"

"In your will. I saw what the documents were. I could hardly keep my eyes from them. And I had seen wills before."

"There is not much time. So I will have the key of the chest. It may soon be wanted."

"Oh, had I not better keep it? Then I should have it in case of need."

"It has its place. It will easily be found. The people in the house will know."

Ninian took the key from a pocket of his purse.

"You would have kept it safe," said Ransom.

"Yes, I am used to matters of trust. I have met with many."

They talked for a while, Ninian with life, and Ransom feebly, with his eyes on his brother. When the others came in to say good-bye, he spoke again to him.

"Stay for a time, Ninian. You want to see your girl. Take them to the gate and come back to me."

"I will stay indeed. It is what I should choose to do. Mother will be glad to hear of it."

Ninian remained for a while at the gate, and returned to the house with his daughter. Ransom was sitting in the same chair, with a difference in himself. He waited until they were seated, and turned to a table and took up a document.

"This is not the will with the later date, Ninian."

"Isn't it? What is it?" said his brother, leaning forward. "Is it some other will? Yes, the date is earlier. How many did you make?"

"The two that you saw. This is the one you should have burnt."

"Yes, I put it on the fire. What of it? This is another?"

"You know which it is. It is the one that should be ashes. I have been to the chest and found it."

"Ah, so you are not so feeble as you claim to be," said Ninian, smiling and shaking his head. "And I am glad of it, Ransom. It is good news. I hope it marks a turning-point in your health. Now what of the wills? Earlier and later! Later and earlier! You have found another and are puzzled by it."

"I have found this one. The one you should have destroyed. I forced myself to reach the chest. I had a feeling that I should do so. And it was a sound one."

"You mistrusted me and my preoccupations? Then why did you give me such a charge?"

"No one would be inattentive in a matter like this."

"Well, did I make a muddle?" said Ninian, drawing in his brows. "Is this the will from the chest or another one?"

"You know there is no other. It is the will I asked you to burn. The will with the earlier date. The will that leaves everything to you. The ashes of the other are in the grate."

"Why do you not do your own work, if you are so equal to it?"

125

"I am equal to nothing. You know my state. This effort is my last."

Ninian remained with his eyes contracted on the will.

"There is nothing amiss with your sight. It is the kind that is good for reading. And you found it good."

"Then there is something amiss with *me*," said Ninian lightly. "There must be, if you say the truth. I must have had a fit of mental blankness. I do have them at times. There is a good deal of strain in my life."

"Then you stand it well. For you had a bout of something else. You read the wills quickly, and as quickly made up your mind. You thought I should not go to the desk, but took the key as a precaution. It was a moral blankness that fell on you. Your brain was doing its work."

"You cannot know what you are implying, Ransom."

"Well, you know. And so does Lavinia. That is enough. And I am implying nothing. I have used plain words."

"I had no time to read two wills. They are the last things to read at a glance. They are so obscured by legal jargon."

"You had time. I measured the minutes. You are familiar with them, as you said. And these were short and clear."

"You have no proof of what you say. None that would count in a court of law."

"It counts in this house. And that is where we are."

"You can't really think that I read them. This is just an act."

"If you can tell me what is in this one, I will let it stand."

Ninian smiled and shook his head.

"Then I will make the other again."

"I do not grudge anyone what you leave her. I should wish the choice to be yours."

"*Her?* And you did not read the wills."

"Oh, it was an obvious guess. Anyone would have made it."

"It was a slip, not a guess. It is hard to keep a hold on

everything. Both of you found it so. Neither of you is versed in ill-doing. Each of you has something of the other."

"Are you versed in it yourself, Ransom? That you prepare the way for it for someone else? It was a poor idea. Are you not ashamed of it?"

"I am not as ashamed as you must be. As I see you are. But we do not leave the matter there. You know what should be said: we have heard you say it; you have done our part. But you have not done your own. You have still to admit the truth."

"Well, then we are a pair, Lavinia and I," said Ninian, putting an arm about his daughter. "She thought it best to prevent my marriage. I thought it best to save her and others from her having powers beyond her. We meant well by each other and by those about us. And if we meant well by ourselves too, well, it was hardly being done for us. We could not help the breach of faith. I see now that she could not help it. Only we know how much we wished we could. We should be drawn closer, if we were not already so close."

"So I have done what I wanted," said his brother.

"It was an unworthy thought, to put temptation in someone's way. To set a trap where it would not be suspected. Neither she nor I would have done it. Our trial was thrust upon us; hers by the hand of chance, mine by that of a brother. Which is the sadder thing?"

"So you are in the pulpit, Ninian? You feel it is your place?"

"You have been in it yourself. And it emerges that it is not yours."

"Because I trusted my brother?"

"Because you did not trust him. And so exposed him to something that assumed trust. I might have read your thought. To fail was simple of me."

"It was your saving grace. It showed you believed in innocence. That means you are not without it."

"And you do not believe in it?"

"Well, have I met it? Here in this kind of place? In many parts it would have no meaning."

"Is everyone to know of this?" said Lavinia.

"When you were in similar trouble, everyone knew," said her uncle.

There was a pause.

"No one need know of it," said Ninian, in a gentle tone. "No one should know. A wrong meaning would be read into it. My motives would be misjudged, as they have already been. There is no point in essential falseness."

"They do say that honesty is best," said Ransom.

"Ransom, you left us for many years. You came back to find welcome, affection, support. Is this your return?"

"Yes, it is. I make it to the girl. You get your reward as her father."

"A part of what you have would give her freedom, if that is what you want."

"So you know what I have," said Ransom, smiling. "You have not learned it from me. And you see what I want. And I see what you do. And if I am the one to have it, well, I am to have nothing else."

"She might marry and take the money from the place. Then you would not have saved it."

"I should have saved her," said Ransom.

"She is too young and untried for such a position."

"She will grow older; and to my mind she has been tried."

"You were to leave everything to me. You came home with that intention."

"It is true. And in the will you preserved, I did so. In the other I left it to Lavinia, to make my test of you a real one. You see I had a certain trust in you. I shall now make a third, leaving it equally between you."

"Oh, leave it all to her. It is what you want. And you have every right to do it. I should rather like to expiate an alien impulse by a natural sacrifice. It puts things in a truer light."

"That is your real word? And your last one?"

"If it were not, should I say it? It would carry too great a risk."

"Then mind you never forget it."

There was a pause.

"Well, shall I destroy this will for you?" said Ninian, in another tone. "It will serve no purpose."

"No, I will not trouble you again. And it will be a foundation for the next. It will supply the legal jargon."

"Well, destroy it in the end. We don't want it lying about."

"No, people might seek a reason for the change."

"No. Your feeling for Lavinia was enough. It is known that you have none for me. But gossip is to be avoided."

"It is the chief of my pleasures," said another voice. "And few people take your view of it."

"Who is at the door?" said Lavinia. "I thought it was ajar."

"Other people were more fortunate," said Ransom. "They knew it was."

"So you have been eavesdropping," said Ninian, in a stern tone.

"No, that is hardly true," said Hugo. "We came back on an errand, and found ourselves rooted to the spot. What else could have happened to us?"

"My word was the right one. Well, I need not mind any exposure of myself. No one is any better placed. I had both reason and temptation on my side. You had neither."

"They had the last," said Ransom. "And it proved too strong. That appears to be its tendency."

"Or what would be its relation to us?" said Lavinia. "It seems to have no other."

"So it is a matter for jest," said Ninian. "Well, it was not for me. I met it and felt I did better to yield to it. It was in a way a temptation not to yield. It would have spared me much."

"I have never felt that sort of temptation," said Hugo. "Perhaps I am above some kinds of it."

"You are silent, Egbert," said Ninian. "What have you to say to me?"

"Very little, Father. It is true that we left you and returned. But we might have stayed, as you did. We could not foresee what was to come."

"You knew we did not see you. You were hidden by the door."

"Not quite," said Hugo. "Lavinia saw it was ajar. I feel that was honest of us."

"I am talking to Egbert," said Ninian.

"I am coming to his help. We were petrified and unable to stir."

"Well, that is almost the truth, Father."

"It could be put in other words. But we will not press on each other. We all learn by our stumbles. I am not above doing so."

"Learning in that way seems hard on other people," said Lavinia. "Does it suggest an inordinate desire for self-improvement?"

"So it is all a jest," said Ninian, again. "Well, I see it has that side. We need only say one more word. We must forget it and keep our own counsel."

"You have the power to say it, Father. I was without it."

"We will share it now," said Ninian, putting his hand on her shoulder.

"Did this have to happen, to bring Father and Lavinia together?" murmured Egbert.

"You need not comment on what is beyond you," said Ninian.

Egbert paused before he answered.

"Is it not soon to take this line with us, Father? We may fall back into our old ways, and shall probably do so. But is it the moment?"

Ninian turned aside and seemed to be hiding a smile, as though seeing his son as a child.

"So you are having a further jest," said Hugo.

"Sometimes one is presented to us," said Ninian, with his lips still unsteady. "But do not provide me with any more. And be sure that is how you see them."

"There is something we can hardly see in that way," said Egbert.

"Yes, yes?" said Ninian, in a perfunctory tone, nodding towards him as if to pacify him. "Well, there is to be silence on these matters to the end. That is agreed upon as best for us. We have all shown our weaker side."

"Well, let it be silence," said Ransom. "Except between those of us here. That is a thing that could not be."

"Should we speak of it to anyone else? To my mother or the children or Miss Starkie? What would you think?"

"That we should speak of it to all of them without the agreement. And with it to most of them in the end."

"Oh, we are not such unscrupulous people," said Ninian, and came to a pause.

"Yes, would it need such unusual unscrupulousness?"

"Shall you speak of it to Teresa, Father?" said Egbert. "It is a thing we should know."

"Surely you do know. I shall not, and neither will anyone who has any goodwill towards her."

"Goodwill can take many forms," said Ransom.

"Well, well, then, gossip if you must. I can keep silence."

"We do not suggest that you will bring up the matter."

"Is Lavina coming home with me?" said Ninian, with a retaliatory note.

"No, this is her home until I die. Then she will do what pleases her."

"She has no young companions here."

"Why do you say it? Egbert is here each day. At home she has no other."

"I hardly think this atmosphere is a good one for her."

"What of the one she was in, when I first saw her? You

talked of long results and altered lives. In a similar place yourself you have asked for silence."

"I may know more than I did. I realise I do know more. I must have the chance to show it. Lavinia will come home with me."

"I am staying here, Father. I also have learned more."

"So you want the inheritance," said Ninian, gently, looking into her face. "You feel you must earn it?"

"She has done so," said Ransom. "We have seen that it is hers."

"And *Father*?" said Ninian, even more gently. "Who is that to you now?"

"Perhaps not anyone. I cannot alter the name. My uncle is something different, something I needed and was without. Something I will hold to while I can."

"Well, may it be long before you lose it. From my heart I wish it. What hope could go deeper in me? So it is goodbye, my daughter. You are still that to me. Your future calls for your thought. Rely on my help, if you need it."

"I don't know why Father should be actually exalted," said Egbert. "Even granting that he cannot be judged."

"He knows that he is not exalted," said Lavinia. "That is what he is dealing with. And with his normal success. If he could fail, he would have done so. To think what our memories will be! And how we shall wish they could fade!"

"I believe I am arranging them for future use," said Hugo.

"You will be talking of it, if you don't take care. Father was right to be afraid of it."

"Well, it does seem that he might suffer some sort of qualm. What would have happened to anyone else in such a place?"

"You can think you would have stood the trial," said Ransom.

"Well, I have pictured myself quietly turning away."

"That is the instinct to dramatise ourselves, that is in all of us."

"Is it? Do you all think of yourselves as coming out well under a trial? I do think it is conceited of you."

"Do you feel you are different from us?"

"Well, yes, when I come out so well."

"In that case he would be different," said Lavinia.

"Here is Father coming back!" said Egbert. "This is a trial."

"Well, it is not as late as I thought," said Ninian. "So there is a word I should say. The subject of wills is never mentioned by people in our sphere of life. No word is said of them until they are revealed. It is a principle that should be observed."

"Like other principles to do with them," said Ransom.

Ninian seemed not to hear.

"And we had better go home together, and not as if we were not on good terms. There is little point in posturing. The wrong I did—and I now see it as a wrong—was done for you all. It does not render me an outcast."

"And if you appear as one, our mother will question you," said Ransom.

"Any more than my daughter was rendered one," continued Ninian, without looking at him. "I remain her father. You remain my son and my brothers."

"I feel I have stood a trial," murmured Hugo. "I don't know how."

The three men left the house, and Ransom turned to his niece.

"I have my own word to say. Remember it, when I am dead. What I leave you will be yours in your own hands. In anyone else's it will be his and used as his own. Do not be wise too late."

CHAPTER X

"So it is over," said Ninian. "The too brief, but we may feel brave life. We do not know its efforts and trials. My brother did not exhibit himself. We owe him our future, the firmness of our roots in the soil. We take it as a gift from him. In a sense he will not die."

"In a poor sense," said Teresa, "as he will not be alive."

"In the sense he chose. He will share our life, as we live it. What he leaves us remains his own. We shall see it as his."

"We see it as Lavinia's. As she sees it, and he saw it."

"Yes, she represents him. We feel it is her place. I take what he gives me, at her hands. He chose her as the intermediary, to add something to the gift. She has the generous part."

"She would have, if it was what you suggest. She will have the one her uncle gave her."

"I take it from both him and her. I see it as a twofold charge. I shall answer to them both."

"And to all of us, Father, if you mean what you say," said Egbert. "But she will have what is hers."

"The power to pass my brother's gift from his hand to mine. It is a cause for pride, a thing to carry with her, an addition to her life."

"And light enough to carry. She would hardly feel the weight."

"I shall not carry it," said Lavinia, in a light tone, not looking at her father. "It is not what Uncle Ransom wished. He did not mean what Father says."

"We know what he meant," said Ninian. "What did he say when he returned to us? What were his first words?"

"Is it second thoughts that are recommended?" said Hugo.

"I am thinking of his last ones, Father. He left all he had to me. You said it was your wish, and held to it when he questioned it. Did your words mean nothing?"

"My brother understood me. We understood each other."

"What did you understand?" said Egbert. "He could have left the money to you."

"The money?" said Ninian, in a dreamy tone. "Yes, that was the form it took. I was to take his gift in the form he chose, in the way he chose. And I do so willingly."

"There is no reason to be unwilling, if your words are true."

Ninian gave a faint smile, and stood as if aloof, with his hand on his chin.

"The money is mine, Father," said Lavinia. "I am not afraid of the word. None of us is afraid of what it means. I shall do as my uncle said."

"Has my daughter changed?" said Ninian.

"She has learned that she is not only your daughter. Perhaps it is a change."

"It is still my marriage?" said Ninian, stooping to look into her face.

"That is in the past. This is the future. And it was never your marriage. It was the difference in yourself. You ask me if I have changed. There was no need to ask it of you. Uncle Ransom said we had something of each other."

"Uncle Ransom said? So that is his place now. So inheritance can do as much as this."

"We do see its forces working," murmured his son.

"To what did the desire for it lead you, Father? I am forced to remind you of it."

"Forced?" said Ninian, gently. "Nothing would force me to recall any similar thing in your life. We have nothing of each other there."

135

"Well, we will leave the matter. There is nothing more to be said."

"The one thing. The word of the future. It is true that it hardly needs saying. That we will work together for the common good, using what is ours to further it. If it is transferred to my name, it will ease your burden. We must not forget your youth. It should be a happy partnership."

"I should once have thought so. But the change has come. And there may be other changes. I may not always be with you. Our lives may go apart."

"If you marry, a portion will be assigned to you. You should be distinguished from the others. Your uncle would wish it, and we should follow his wish."

"We know his last decision. That I should have the whole. And I have a legal right to it."

"Legal? I was thinking of the moral one," said Ninian, so incidentally as hardly to utter the words.

"I am going to marry, Father. The money may not be too much. I have no knowledge of such things. I am marrying a poor man."

"She is," said Hugo, moving forward. "And a man who is nothing else, except old and over-familiar. I hope it is true that frankness is disarming."

There was a pause before Ninian spoke.

"You do not mean you want to marry my daughter?"

"What did you think I meant?"

"I could not believe my ears. I do not now."

"We have found it hard to believe ours. But ears seldom really deceive."

"Lavinia, you have been carried away. The sense of having money has upset you. You did not think of the effect on other people. This is not the way to use it. I beg you to think again."

"I have thought, Father. This is what we both have wished. And now we can have it."

"If Hugo—if your uncle was worthy of the name of a man, you could have had it before."

"Well, of course I am not that, Ninian."

"It is an unthinkable thing. It is unnatural and unfit. There can only be one opinion."

"I never like things that are described as natural. And we should not be the slaves of opinion."

"We can be the slaves of things that I will not state."

"I am sure you are wise, Ninian. Then I will not either."

"What is your feeling for Lavinia herself, apart from them."

"You must know there are things that are never put into words."

"As you have said, there is nothing in your favour. Your best years are behind. You are old compared with her. You might be her father."

"No, Ninian, I could not take your place."

"And you are almost a relation. She sees you as an uncle."

"No, not now, Father," said Lavinia. "I have not since I was a child."

"And how long is that? And how long has this been threatening? Since the promise of your uncle's money?"

"Long before with me," said Hugo. "As soon as it could be with her. And now it can be realised."

"You would not work for your wife, like other men?"

"Ninian, I am what I am. That is what you have against me. If I were not, you would have nothing. And if I were as other men, Lavinia might not have accepted me."

"You talk as if recognising your failings altered them."

"Well, you might feel you had never liked me so well."

"So it is not a serious thing. I thought you could not mean it."

"It is serious, Father," said Lavinia. "You should not find it so strange. When you resolved to marry yourself, you meant it."

137

"Marriage means a loss," said Teresa. "In this case it is a double one. Are we to make it greater than it is?"

"It will be nice to be missed," said Hugo. "Though it seems it ought not to be. And I never know how people know about it."

"Will you live far away?" said Egbert.

"Near enough to be in touch with you. Lavinia made it a condition. I am in her power, as I have really always been."

"We can see the change," said Ninian. "Lavinia, think while there is time. You are in early youth. You have met few men. You must wait for the chances of your life. And your uncle should know it."

"Well, I did know I was not a chance," said Hugo.

"You have taken one. It seems it must be recognised. How great do you mean it to be? How much of Ransom's legacy do you see as yours?"

"None of it. It is Lavinia's."

"So the whole. But how does she see it? It was destined for the place, to ensure its future. She can only feel a part of it is hers."

"I see it all as mine, Father. My uncle would have wished me to have it. He felt you should abide by your words. When people do something for themselves, they do say someone else would have wished it. But it may be the truth."

"Truth does not need a veil," said Ninian, gravely. "So we do not see it here."

"It has needed one in your case and mine. We found it, when it did not have it."

"What does Egbert feel?" said Ninian. "He will come after me here. It will be a poor inheritance, when they all take their share. My brother meant it to be otherwise."

"Not at the end, Father. He left all he had to Lavinia. He was in no doubt."

"Was he not? He would have kept a will in my favour, if

I could have fulfilled a certain condition. I could not, as matters were. But it showed his mind."

"I remember, Father," said Lavinia.

"So we should not take this will as essentially his true one," said Ninian, continuing at once. "It is a chance that it stood as it did."

"The matter is settled," said Egbert. "Lavinia takes what is hers. We should all do the same. We must not betray disappointment. We should not feel it."

"That is said," said Ninian, gently. "But why should we not betray it? We betray our other feelings. Of course I am disappointed. I might be a lesser man, if I were not. I hoped to improve my forefathers' land, to benefit my family, to safeguard your future. They are a man's natural wishes. I am not ashamed of them."

"Well, I am of mine," said Hugo. "I want to live on inherited means and consider only one person besides myself. I knew I was a lesser man. But perhaps I hardly knew how much."

"Come in, Miss Starkie," said Ninian, raising his voice. "Come in and bring your flock. We have an engaged couple to present to you. It is a thing you did not expect."

"I did not, Mr. Middleton. What is on foot? Are they acting a play? Where are the two protagonists?"

"It may turn out in that way. It is serious at the moment. Let the leading characters come forward and speak for themselves."

"Why, Lavinia, what a solemn face! You don't look much of a bride. I know people weep at weddings. But it is usually the bride's mother, I am told."

"Lavinia's mother would weep at this one," said Ninian.

"Why, what is it? It is not a serious thing? Is there a real bridegroom? Not Lavinia's uncle? No, it cannot be."

"Hugo is not my uncle," said Lavinia. "He is not Grandma's son. He and I are not related."

"I know you are not. But it is almost the same. It does not make much difference."

"Well, I would hardly say that," said Ninian, smiling. "But in a sense it is true. They are too much uncle and niece to be a success as anything else."

"Do you give your consent, Mr. Middleton? I can hardly think it."

"I have not been asked for it. And I realise you have not. They may have been afraid of our answer."

"They may well have been of mine. I could not pretend to approve. And Lavinia is too young to take such a step. I cannot but feel you should oppose it."

"You can hardly suppose I have not done so. But I am powerless."

"In a legal sense. But not in any other."

"In every sense. I admit I hardly knew it."

There was a silence, broken by Leah.

"Is he marrying her because she is rich now? He didn't want to before."

"He must answer you himself," said her father.

"I have always wanted to," said Hugo. "But I was too poor to think of it."

"That has a better sound," said Ninian. "But is there any real difference?"

"Yes, there is a real one. But not the one you mean."

"Was it hard to be silent, Uncle?" said Agnes, taking a step forward, with brighter eyes.

"Well, it was at times."

"So there has been a romance, and we did not know."

"If there had been, you would have known," said Ninian.

"Hardly at her age," said Miss Starkie. "That is no proof of anything. We may wish it was."

"But none of us at any age knew. Did you know, Egbert?"

"I feel now that I did in a way, Father."

"Oh, we all feel it now. That is saying nothing."

"Lavinia, think of the future," said Miss Starkie. "You might be left a widow when you were still young."

"I should otherwise always be single. I would not marry any other man."

"Do you not congratulate me, Miss Starkie?" said Hugo.

"I have long done so in your character of uncle. This new one is too much for me. I cannot deny it. The disparity in age speaks for itself."

"It could have saved itself the trouble," said Lavinia.

"And if it is not an intrusive question, what of the material problems? You have always lived in your brother's house."

"In this house. Ninian is not my brother. And not at his expense. I am not quite without means. And Lavinia will have what her uncle leaves."

"But that surely passes to her father. Whether or no there is a will. Forgive me, if I am wrong."

"It would be harder to forgive you, if you were right," said Ninian. "No, the money is not to be mine. My brother left it to Lavinia. We will not talk about whose it will be."

"It can be put in a word, Father. It will belong to Hugo and me."

"But you will not act in haste," said Miss Starkie. "Remember the life behind you. You have always felt more for your father."

"Not always. Not for some time. As you imply, it is in the past."

"We are thrust aside, Miss Starkie. We are in a similar place. We must be content to have served our purpose."

"I should be indeed. But I feel I can hardly have served it. I did not look for this. It is no good to deny it."

"It does seem too late," said Hugo.

"I am hardly myself, Mr. Hugo. I hope you don't misunderstand me."

"No, you have taken no risk of it."

"You feel with me, Teresa?" said Ninian.

"For my own sake rather than theirs. This may settle two lives that needed it. But it is hard to be sure."

"Well, we wish them well. There is no need to say it. We must put aside our own feelings. They are after all a part of ourselves. We will go forward with them, hoping for them everything, grudging them nothing. I say the last for myself. Lavinia will believe me and see me as her father."

"Yes, I will, Father," said Lavinia, moving to his arms, as he held them out to her.

"Father can't marry Lavinia," said Leah, standing with her eyes on them.

"Of course he cannot," said Miss Starkie. "What a foolish speech!"

"I said that he couldn't, not that he could. And I never know why they can't."

"They would, if the law allowed it," said Hengist. "Or why does there have to be a law?"

"And he is married to *her*," said Leah.

"I am not going to say anything," said Miss Starkie. "You need not expect it."

"She doesn't want us to say *Mamma*. She thinks we don't feel in that way to her. And she doesn't mind."

"I am frustrating your efforts, Miss Starkie," said Teresa.

"We saw the need for them then. I think it cannot be denied."

"I fear you have striven unsupported."

"Do they call you anything, Mrs. Middleton?" said Miss Starkie, suggesting the result of this.

"Well, we rejected everything and were left with nothing."

"Well, if that is a satisfactory conclusion!" said Miss Starkie, forcing a brisk tone.

Selina entered the room, and at once looked from face to face.

"We have news for you, Mother," said Ninian. "I

believe you feel we have. It is at once near to you and far from your thoughts. You may have some inkling of it. You are a hard person to surprise."

"Do not lead up to it, my son. Let me have it in a word. You must know it."

"This uncle and niece are no longer to be what they are. What they are to be I hesitate to say. It may be a shock to you"

"If they want to be married, they can't be," said Selina, in a shriller tone. "I have seen it coming and thought my eyes deceived me. I have heard and disbelieved my ears. It cannot be. It is a wrong, unnatural thing."

"It is natural, Grandma," said Egbert, "for a man and a woman in the same home to be attracted to each other."

"No, that happens when they are in different homes. The attraction of closeness is the result of it. It dies in the open. When they were in it, they would find it dead."

"It will live and grow in me," said Hugo.

"You should not have let it arise. You knew all there was against it. Look at it as others will. Marrying a virtual niece, when she inherits a fortune? It will tell one tale."

"To us it tells another. We are only concerned with our own."

"You are holding your eyes from the future. You would live in the atmosphere, breathe the air, hear the voices you always had. And would feel you always would. All your life as well as hers. All her young life as well as yours. Ninian, can you not prevent it? You are her father."

"I could only use words, as you have. And you see the use of those. Miss Starkie did the same, with the same result, that is with none."

"And she represents the many. They will all say the one thing. We shall always hear it."

"Try not to be troubled, Mother. They are hardly doing wrong. They are unwise and are likely to rue it. And we can hardly see Hugo as we did. But we must

143

accept what we cannot alter. And do all in our power to help them."

"Help them? To the harm of each other's lives? To the undoing of your daughter's. And what help is in your power? You are a shadow on the scene. You appear to choose the part. We must suppose it is yours."

"It is mine. I am nothing. I can do and say no more."

"Well, I can," said Selina. "I can both do and say it. I can betray my husband and reveal the truth. I will tell you a thing you were never to know, that no one has ever known. Hugo is your father's son. That is why he was adopted. That is why he has something of his own. That is how he came to be one of us."

There was a pause.

"Tell us the whole," said Ninian.

"It happened before you remember. When Hugo was in his infancy. Your father determined to adopt him, and would not be denied. He said he was the orphan son of a friend, and would say no more. I did not question him; I had no need; I accepted what could not be helped. I had no doubt that the boy was his. I have none now. His feeling for him proved it, both then and as time went by. We ostensibly took him as a companion for Ninian, when we thought we might not have another child. It was a natural thing to do, and aroused no question."

"Hugo is Lavinia's uncle?" said Ninian.

"Her uncle by half-blood. Your half-brother. Your father's son."

"They say that truth is best," said Egbert. "I wonder what anything else would be."

"Truth is needed here," said Ninian. "We are forced to welcome it. But it was wise to keep the secret. We must all keep it now."

"It has been kept through your lives. It was kept even from me. It was neither right nor wrong, but it was best."

"It is the truth, Grandma?" said Lavinia. "You feel it is?"

"As far as I can tell it, my child. I wish at this moment that it was not."

"Mother," said Hugo, "you have done well by me."

"I feared to do ill. I would not fail my husband or your helplessness. In doing what we must, we come to do more. I came to care for you. And I have had return."

"It is strange news," said Ninian. "It ends the threat that was on us. It must do other things. We shall get used to the knowledge."

"I shall not," said Hugo. "To me there is no change. And to Lavinia there will be none."

"That is not a thing to say," said Ninian.

"It is what we both of us feel."

"In a way we are closer," said Lavinia.

"You are," said her father, gravely. "The natural tie is strong. Your feeling for your uncle had a truer basis than you knew. You can recognise it between yourselves."

"We can marry and live as brother and sister," said Hugo. "As our real relation is not known."

"What next?" said Ninian sharply. "First an uncle, then a suitor, now a brother! What will your next thought be?"

"I will tell you. We can live as what we have been, as adopted uncle and niece. The difference in years, that looms so large, can help us there."

"But why make the change, as you have not made it before? Oh, of course, there is the money."

"Yes, of course. No one can live on nothing. Ransom knew it, when he set Lavinia free."

There was a pause before Ninian spoke again.

"She may use her freedom. The choice is hers. What do you say, my daughter?"

"We might do it, Father. We could for a time. But it might not be for always. It would not be the same for Hugo. There might be a different end."

"Say *Uncle Hugo*, as you always have, like the brave girl you are," said Ninian.

"Well, *Uncle Hugo*. What difference does it make? If we lived as uncle and niece, I should have to say it."

There was a silence.

"So it has made the difference," said Hugo.

"And it makes another," said Ninian, bending towards his daughter. "It restores our partnership, our power to help the future. It gives back much."

"And from you it takes nothing," said Teresa.

There was again a silence.

"Hugo, I may welcome you as a brother?" said Ninian, holding out his hand. "You will let me be glad of it in itself. I almost wish Ransom had known."

"He knew," said Selina. "I had to share the knowledge. I could not carry it alone. After your father died, he knew. Until then I felt I did share it."

"He kept the secret," said Ninian. "It was a thing he could do. So it was the deserter who had your confidence."

"Not because he deserted. I could have loved him better, and told him more."

"I do not grudge him his place. I hope I grudge nothing to anyone. I am sometimes misjudged."

"So are many of us. So was he."

"Are we sure of the truth?" said Lavinia. "Sure beyond doubt? Is there any real proof?"

"Your grandfather's words. That the boy had a claim he could neither forget nor reveal. It meant what it did."

"Have you my birth certificate?" said Hugo.

"I had nothing to do with your birth. Your mother died at the time. I have never pursued the events. It would have ended in nothing. Or rather in the one thing."

"I will take every step to find out the truth. To prove or disprove your theory. There may be some hope."

"There is none. The truth is what it must be. It can be nothing else."

"So Uncle Hugo is really our uncle," said Egbert. "It seems to make a difference, to be a strange, deep thing."

"We are not to know it," said Selina.

"Or speak of it again," said Ninian. "So already that has to be said. There are ears everywhere."

There were some outside the door.

"It is a thunderbolt, Cook," said Ainger. "The old master! Who would have thought it?"

"Not you or I, unless we forgot ourselves."

"So I am better in a way than he was."

"There are other points of difference that we might be alive to."

"Well, it seems the first can be last, and the last first."

"Ainger, you should curb your tongue. It carries you onward."

"It is not so much of a failing."

"You are confident of yourself. No sin is venial."

"You never lose your hope of me, do you?"

"Well, if I am struck by glimpses, it is not for you to express it."

"What is it all about?" said another voice.

"You need not put questions, James. You go beyond yourself."

"You can keep to your place," said Ainger. "You are beginning to grace it."

"Am I better than I was?" said James, with his face in a sudden glow.

"You are on the upward grade, James," said Cook, in a severe tone. "But do not overestimate it and fall backwards. That is a snare."

"And go and do something useful," said Ainger, yawning.

"Yes, sir," said James, his step, as he sprang away, causing Cook to start and glance aside.

"So you were ashamed of what you were doing," said Ainger with a grin.

"Well, gossip is no ground for pride. Though we all stoop at times."

"We don't have to stoop so much, when we are already low."

"I do not apply the term to myself. Nor is it used by others."

"A thing I should not choose to be, is a governess."

"Well, the choice might not fall on you, Ainger. You might be seen as lacking on some points."

"I hope we shall listen to some further revelations."

"There is no need for downrightness. Overhearing is a word."

"It is hardly the right one."

"Well, we can strain at a gnat."

"I should call it swallowing a camel."

"You need not cap me, Ainger. My words may stand. And we have talked enough. There are signs."

"Wouldn't you like to be on the other side of the door?"

"If I cannot deny it, it is where I should not be," said Cook, as she walked away.

CHAPTER XI

"Has the breakfast hour been changed?" said Ninian.

"You know it has not," said Teresa. "We are observing the usual one. The others are late this morning."

"Not late in coming down. I have ended that. They are loitering outside the house, expecting us to wait for them."

"Well, they will be disappointed, and will not expect it again."

"I am a solitary creature," said Ninian, trying to smile. "Steering my course alone! Well, I should be used to it."

"They will soon be coming in."

Ninian raised his shoulders and dropped them in easy despair.

"Oh, I believe Hugo has returned! They have gone out to welcome him and hear his news."

"Then they may as well stay out," said Ninian, with a faint, frowning movement of his eyes towards Ainger. "Breakfast will be over before they come in."

"Yours will be, if it proceeds at that rate."

Ninian put aside his plate and turned to the next with an air of quiet attention.

"Shall I bring something hot, ma'am?" said Ainger, as he removed the plate.

"No, there is no need," said Ninian, without looking up.

"Ainger was speaking to me," said his wife.

"Well, I have answered for us both. You need not trouble."

"Mr. Hugo has travelled at night, sir. He will want something."

"There does not seem any sign of it. Perhaps he has had breakfast."

"No, sir. The train has not long been in. He must be tired and hungry."

"He can hardly be the last," said Ninian, half-laughing. "Or he would be more anxious to remedy the matter."

"He seems to have something to tell, that is detaining them, sir."

"It does appear to have that result."

"The mistress is with them, sir," said Ainger, as if this was significant.

"Oh, I am glad she is equal to it. We need not keep you any longer."

"No, sir," said Ainger, with a readiness that disposed of any desire to remain.

As footsteps were heard, Ninian rose from the table, brushed his napkin across his lips and went to the door. Encountering the group, he waited for them to pass, and pursued his way.

"Stay, Father," said Egbert. "Uncle Hugo has his news to tell."

"Nothing urgent, I gather. There was no hurry to impart it."

"We were spellbound by it. It may have far results. You must wait and hear it."

"I have waited," said his father.

"Tell him, Hugo," said Selina, sinking into a chair and ignoring her son's mood. "A few words will be enough."

"You will hear it, Ninian?" said Hugo.

"Yes, if it concerns me. It seemed that it did not."

"You will feel it does. It is what I had a hope it might be. A hope I hardly dared to frame. I have found out the truth about myself. And I am not your father's son. I have traced the events to my birth, pursued the evidence, followed every track, and reached a certain result. My father was a widowed friend of your father's, whose death your father caused in a moment of youthful violence. He suffered a lifetime's remorse, never uttered a word of the truth, preferred any account of his adoption of me to the true one. That is the whole story. You see its meaning for me. I am not related to Lavinia. Our future is free and clear. You will rejoice with us, if you are a natural father."

There was a pause.

"The certainty is absolute?" said Ninian. "As a natural father I must ask that."

"It may be, my son," said Selina. "The account agrees with what I know. There may be no room for doubt. There must be proof, if you want it and will follow it. But Hugo is prepared."

"As a natural father I am disturbed," said Ninian, in a lighter tone. "There is the risk that the threat of this marriage may return. But I hope it is only a natural father's uneasiness."

"A threat? It is a certainty," said Hugo. "Of course it will return. That was the object of my effort, and is its reward. I thought you understood."

"I feared it," said Ninian, as if to himself. "It flashed into my mind as I heard. We must hope the danger will pass."

"What have you against the marriage?"

Ninian gave a sigh, as if at a threadbare question.

"I will say one thing once. Your holding Lavinia to a life that denies her youth. That is, the sacrifice of it. Surely it is enough."

"She will make the life for us both. I am willing to share what is hers. I am free from the pride that would satisfy itself at her expense."

"Well, would not everything be at her expense?" said Ninian, with a little laugh. "It is true that you are without pride. But the words are empty ones. It is too late for the change'"

"It is the time for it, as you know. And I shall not touch what is not mine. Lavinia will deal with it."

"But there would only be what was yours," said Ninian, contracting his brows. "What was hers is put to other purposes. Both you and she know it."

"There has been no change. She has taken no legal step. It has simply to remain in her hands."

"Yes, we must ask that, Father," said Lavinia.

"But what do you ask?" said Ninian, with a bewildered air. "It cannot be withdrawn now. Its uses are mapped out and settled as your uncle wished."

"Nothing has been done," said Teresa. "It has not been put to any use. Lavinia sees it as hers."

"This series of steps!" said Ninian, smiling. "And the same money! How many times can it be given away?"

"It is not to be given, Father. We have our freedom again. I must have what is mine and use it. I want to give Hugo another life, and to share it with him. You think there will be nothing new in it. But for us there will."

"No, my dear," said Ninian, gravely. "I must assert my authority. For your sake, for my sake, for the sake of us all. But for your sake the most."

"You can only make it hard for me. You know the truth."

"Did she mean to have everything then?" said Ninian, with gentle raillery. "She wanted to give a thing and take a thing, like the wicked man in the rhyme? Well, it does not trouble her father. He understands his natural girl."

"Do you mean you would use the money for yourself?"

"No, of course I do not. I have said what I shall do. Use it as my brother wished, before illness clouded his mind. That wish is sacred to me, as his real one. And I shall save you from a fatal step. That wish is *my* real one, my dear."

"I can hardly believe you, Father. Is this the man you have been?"

"It is the man I am. The man who will suffer misjudgement to save you. In other words your father."

"There would be many other words," said Hugo. "Happily there will be no cause for them."

"Hugo, I have lost you as a brother. Am I to lose you in every sense?"

152

"No, I am to be nearer, Ninian. I will try to be a son to you."

"So you have given your answer," said Ninian, without a smile.

"You are sure, my son?" said Selina, in a voice that sounded far away. "The money is apart from the marriage. It is not all one thing."

"Mother, our thoughts should be on you," said Ninian, turning as if in compunction. "I spoke of a brother. You are feeling you have lost a son. A long tie is broken."

"No, I am glad to know the truth. I am glad it is what it is. Glad that your father never turned from me. I wish I had always known."

"Have you always known, Grandma?" said Lavinia.

"I have known nothing," said Selina, dreamily. "I could not ever be sure. I was not sure about what I said. It might have been true. I often thought it was. You must have known I could not be sure."

"Why did you put it as a certainty?"

"I wanted to save you," said Selina, in a deeper tone, leaning forward and looking into her face. "Hugo does not care for you enough. You are a person who inspires deep feeling. That is a thing we don't explain. He has not the depth in him that you have. I wanted to save you both. And I may do it, if I go on thinking. I have my thoughts."

"Well, I must take up my cross," said Ninian. "I must be a resolute father. It is not an easy course."

"Nor a credible one," said Egbert. "And it can avail you nothing."

"It is a question of our lives, Father," said Lavinia. "If we are living for ourselves, it is time we did. I am not a lofty character. That is too well recognised for it to be expected."

"The past is forgotten. Anyhow by your father. Why do you remind people of it?"

"It is what you are doing," said Teresa.

153

"We cannot prove you are not honest, Father," said Egbert.

"And you want to prove it?" said Ninian, gently. "It is a sad thing to have to say. More and more I see where the power should lie. The suspected person may be the one above suspicion. I am not afraid to claim the place. My mind is open to you all. I have hidden nothing. I have nothing to hide."

"If only he would hide some of it!" murmured Egbert.

"Now the one thing has been found out," said Hugo. "You intended that to be hidden."

"Tell me what that is," said Selina, in a petulant tone. "I have heard whispers about it. I have asked before. I should not ask, if I did not want to know."

"It was to do with Ransom's will," said Hugo. "As Ninian's activities tend to be."

"Anyone who speaks of my will may get nothing from it," said Selina, nodding her head. "I shall know who it is. It is the kind of thing I know. But I have thought about it. I have done one thing. And I am thinking of another."

"Mother, what are you saying?" said Ninian. "Yours is a life we never imagine ended."

"It will not be left to imagination. No one knows what it is to be a memory. No one will ever know."

"Mother, you are tired. Our talk has been too much. And it has been a waste of words. Most of them were better unsaid."

"I am often tired," said Selina, putting her hand to her head. "But not in this way before. I have heard without knowing anything. And that is not a thing I do. It is as if I were someone else. It all goes by as though it had no meaning."

"It has not had much," said Ninian. "You chose your absent moment well. It was wise not to try to follow it."

"I could not follow. That is what I said. It may not have been worth it. But you all seemed to feel it was."

"There are the children," said Ninian. "I will call them in. They will be a change for you."

"A change?" said Selina, drawing in her brows. "I often see them."

"They will help you to forget what you should not have heard. Their world is still an honest one."

"Agnes and Hengist and Leah!" said Selina, sitting up, and then breaking off with an empty look in her eyes.

"Come in and talk to your grandmother," said Ninian. "Say something to interest her."

"Did you not hear what your father said?" said Miss Starkie, speaking from safety herself.

"I did not hear," said Selina, shaking her head. "Not so that I knew what it was."

"Grandma, you are tired," said Agnes. "You don't seem like yourself."

"She told you to say it," said Selina, looking at Miss Starkie.

"Oh, I could have managed better than that, Mrs. Middleton."

"You tell us a good deal about yourself. It never comes to an end."

"Leah, you can say something," said Miss Starkie, hesitating to go any further herself.

"So you put it on to her. That is not doing so well. And it is the other who says the right thing, and knows it is better than the wrong one."

"It might not be true," said Hengist.

"Would you like me to die?" said Selina, as if catching his meaning.

"No, I don't think so. Why should I?"

"You know you would not," said Miss Starkie, hardly able to fall short of this.

"When I am dead, will they remember me?" said Selina, to herself.

"Yes, we shall," said Hengist. "Father will be sad, and so will Lavinia. And that will remind us."

155

"You would not need reminder," said Miss Starkie.

"I only said we should have it."

"Tell us what you think of our real question, Grandma," said Egbert.

"You mean the money? It must happen as it will. They all want everything. We don't know who should have it."

"There are always different claims," said Ninian. "And always the one real one."

"You must not be selfish, Ninian," said Selina, as if saying an accustomed word to a child.

"That is true. I have a chance to serve them all. I must not lose it."

"It is easy to give what falls into your hands."

"It might be easier to keep it. But I am not one of your people who want everything."

"You always seem to have it," said his mother.

"And we seldom do that without wanting it," said Hugo.

"Hugo, I have never said what I hesitate to say now. This house is mine. I have never grudged you a place in it. You have not found the talk of my grudging true. Do not force it to be so now."

"Your parents gave me the place and enough to keep it. I have cost you nothing."

"Money!" said Ninian, sadly. "So there is nothing else. No affection, no sharing of deeper things, no place in family life. And I must answer your words with my own. I have not gained anything either. Not that I wished to gain."

"You knew I had nothing over. Anything I had, you would have taken. You have given the proof."

"You all want it all," said Selina. "And Ninian has the most. He has had the chance, and that is what it is. No one gives until he must. We find that is true when we make a will. I have tried to do it wisely. And I think I have been wise. But you all want everything, and no one can have it or give it. I will go now."

She rose from her chair, and as Ninian went to help her, looked up into his face.

"I wish it was yours, my son. It would be better so. But if it is not, you will give it to them. They will have what is theirs."

"Yes, yes, I will," said Ninian, stooping over her. "It is mine, but I will not remember. I will say no more, and that means that it is given. And that it is taken. That is the certain thing. And I should not have used it for myself. It is other people who give. And it is my daughter who takes. I am content, if others are."

"I am content," said Hugo to Lavinia. "But I did not know I should be so ashamed of it. Can it be true that self-denial is its own reward? Even when it is forced on us."

Selina went to the door, and her son followed with his eyes on her, as if oblivious of anything else. Miss Starkie manœuvred her charges in front of them, and urged them to the stairs.

"Why is there a hurry?" said Hengist, on an upper floor.

"You might not have known what to say to your grandmother. She is overtired."

"She didn't seem to like you, did she?" said Leah.

"She is not herself to-day," said Miss Starkie, in explanation of this.

"She seemed to be herself," said Hengist.

"No one who cared for her could think so."

"Do you care for her yourself?" said Leah.

"I appreciate what she is. Of course she is not my grandmother."

"No. She couldn't be as old as that."

"Well, it would be possible," said Miss Starkie, seeing no reason to disregard the truth.

"Would it?" said Hengist. "You haven't even any parents."

"Well, they did not live to be old."

"Did your being a governess break their hearts?"

"And bring their grey hairs with sorrow to the grave?"

157

said Leah. "That would have been a pity, if they weren't even grey."

"What kind of a person is Grandma?" said Hengist. "Very good or very bad?"

"She is good, of course. No one can be perfect," said Miss Starkie, forced to a reservation in Selina's case.

"Why isn't she perfect? Because she does not like you?"

"We are good friends when she is herself."

"Can people be good friends, when one is despised and rejected of the other?"

"You don't attend to what I say," said Miss Starkie, with justification.

"I have always been Grandma's favourite," said Agnes.

"When people are that, they sometimes deserve to be," said Miss Starkie, tired of too little effort in this direction.

"Leah and I would not stoop to fawn on people."

"Some people's level does not admit of much stooping."

"She means our level is low," said Leah.

"Well, so is everyone's. Only some people have more power. People are really all the same."

"Indeed they are not," said Miss Starkie. "There can be a great difference."

"Well, Grandma said they were," said Leah. "She kept on saying it."

"I should not remember what she said to-day," said Miss Starkie, in favour of a general forgetfulness.

"Do you mean what she said about you?" said Hengist.

"No. What did she say? I hardly recall it. I meant what she said about you, if I am to speak the truth."

"We might not recall that."

"No. It is best to put it all out of your minds," said Miss Starkie, on a sympathetic note.

"If Grandma dies, wouldn't you have to remember her last words to you?" said Leah.

"I am afraid I already forget them. And we hope they are not her last."

"Does she really hope it?" said Leah.

CHAPTER XII

"It is a strange feeling," said Ninian. "To be no longer a son. It is the deepest of all changes. It has torn up my roots, thrown me solitary into the future. It will be hard to feel anchored again."

"I should be proud if it did so much to me," said Hugo. "The part it has done shows me what the whole must be."

"Proud? I am lonely, bereft, uncertain. In a measure it must be so with you all."

"There is a cause for pride, Father," said Lavinia. "To be such things beyond a measure."

"Ah, you would once have been with me. At a time not so far away. Now I must see you move to a distance. Well, in a sense I shall go with you."

"Why do you keep saying how proud you are, Father?" said Egbert. "We can all see it."

"To me it is no occasion for jest. It is the first when the voice will not sound, that I have always heard. And the first of many. That is the heavy part."

"We all miss Grandma, and shall always miss her. It hardly needs to be said."

"Then it has had good measure," said Hugo. "And from you both."

"Hardly the same," said Ninian. "Words are not so powerless. Other words arise from other feeling. They come from within. My future is a sea of change. My mother gone from me, my daughter going, my brother that to me no longer."

"All our lives are changing," said Teresa. "Even Leah can hardly say there will be no difference."

"You and Ninian will have each other," said Hugo.

"That foolish thing that is said, when that is all people have. As if they did not know it! It is the whole trouble."

"It is not only trouble," said Ninian, smiling at Teresa. "Or it is trouble shared and therefore less."

"Did Grandma leave a will?" said Egbert. "I suppose there is no doubt of it."

"No doubt at all," said Ninian, sounding surprised and looking at his son. "She left nothing undone that needed doing."

"Do you know the terms, Father? No doubt you helped her to make it."

"No doubt again. She would not have been without my help. I was never without hers."

"I daresay she knew her own mind."

"There is again no doubt," said Ninian, smiling. "But I have not thought of the will since it was made. She and I were of the same mind. That is what I remember."

"Well, it disposes of everything else," said Hugo. "It must be a calming memory."

"I have other memories," said Ninian.

"Do you feel she had a happy life?" said Teresa.

"A full one. And that must mean some losses. She met them with her own courage."

"I am glad I am a coward," said Hugo. "Courage is another strain added to the rest. It does nothing for anyone."

"Hers did much for me," said Ninian. "I am the better for it. I found it uplifting."

"Can everything be Grandma's fault?" murmured Egbert.

"Pride should go before a fall," said Hugo. "But it does not seem to."

"Yes, I am the better," said Ninian, looking at him. "And it should also be true of you. You know her mind, and will follow it. You could have no truer aim."

"You don't mean I should give up my marriage? So that she will not have died in vain?"

"What else should I mean? I have not changed. And you know she had not."

"We have not either. So a religion would have had its use. We could have said that she now understood."

"You know she understood this. And you know you yourself understand it. What does my honest daughter feel?"

"Not that we should follow a wish, now she is dead, that we did not follow in her life. What would it do for her?"

"What would it do for you? That would be her thought."

"It could only be ours, Father. She has no thoughts now."

"You know I represent her. In so far as our thoughts would be the same, they should be hers to you."

"She should be here to keep a hand on you," said Hugo.

"Yes, she should be here," said Ninian. "But I feel the hand."

"We shall all feel it," said Egbert. "And partly as she meant us to. We should know about things, Father. They will have to go on without her."

"Without her! It will not seem like going on."

"It is better than a standstill. We must learn what the changes are to be."

"To-day?" said his father.

"Well, it is a difficult day to live. We may as well make some use of it. It will leave a better memory. And I need some light on the future. We have depended on Grandma's money."

"Some of it was your grandfather's, and comes direct to me," said Ninian, with his eyebrows slightly raised. "She has left what was her own also to me, knowing it would pass to her grandchildren. There are the natural bequests to dependants. And there is a legacy to your uncle, and a message to him added in her own hand on the day before she died. That has no legal significance. It will have the more for him."

"Then you have seen the will, Father. You said you had not thought of it, since it was made."

"And I have not," said Ninian, smiling. "It is not I, who thought of it to-day. When I put it out for the lawyer, I caught sight of the message at the end. It is not embodied in the will. You are not my friend, my boy."

"Tell me the message," said Hugo. "Of course that is all I should think of."

"It is short and simple. It stresses the meaning of the legacy. She felt it lessened the advantage of your marriage, and she trusted it would prevent it."

"She did not make it a condition?"

"No, the message has no legal force. It comes simply from her to you. She felt it was enough."

"She could have made it a condition, if she had meant it to be one," said Lavinia.

"No, my dear, she was above it," said Ninian, at once. "It would have been to fail you and your uncle and herself. He has her word of trust. He needs nothing more."

"But she knew I was unworthy of trust," said Hugo. "So the word means nothing."

"It means what it says. What else could it mean? Why should she have written it in her last weakness?"

"She did not tell you about it?"

"No, her strength was gone. She used the last of it for you."

"I wish she had had just a little less. She did always have a great deal."

"We must forget the message," said Lavinia. "There is no middle course."

"Forget it?" said her father. "Her last words, her last wish? They mean no more than that to you? Did you act a part with her?"

"No, and I will not now. We cannot fulfil the wish. So it is best not to think of it."

"Best?" said Ninian, keeping his brows raised.

"Yes, for us. For her we cannot do anything."

"Well, you will do nothing. You still act a part."

"I may as well show my full self," said Hugo. "It will cause no surprise. Did you see the amount of the legacy?"

"I did not see the will. I already knew the amount. I had my mother's confidence."

"Ninian, would you force me to go further?"

"You would hardly wish to to-day. It is no occasion for facts and figures."

"It is only the one little figure. Of course it is not a large one. And it is in your mind. I shall be no worse than you are."

"It was not, until you recalled it. What was in my mind was her thought and hope for you. For to-day is not that enough?"

"It is too much. All I want is the one little thing that you would not count. And I will not count it either. I must know it, to dismiss it from my mind."

"The legacy is in safe investments, and can be estimated," said Ninian, in a full, cold tone, naming the sum. "It renders you independent of me and my home and my daughter. You see its significance."

"I do. I can marry Lavinia without any feeling of guilt."

"*Without* any?" said Ninian.

"Without that of supposedly sordid motives. I shall be able to do my part."

"You can forget my mother's message to you?"

"Yes, if you never remind me of it. Let it be a pact between us."

"It might be the more remembered."

"Well, that would not matter so much."

"I could not have believed the occasion would be taken in this spirit," said Ninian, as if to himself.

"Neither could I. Things are never as bad as we expect. This one is not."

"You mean the legacy means more to you, than the woman who was your virtual mother?"

"The legacy is all I can have. And all I can have of her. And it binds me closer to her. You can see it does."

"But you would let it ensure the thing she meant it to prevent?"

"It must be one of life's inconsistencies. Or perhaps it was one of hers. She would have been above mere consistency. I remember that she was."

"Hugo, would it not be better to appear to be serious to-day?"

"I am really serious. I don't dare to seem to be. I am so afraid of you."

"I would rather have a plain word than all this evasive irony, if that is what it is."

"I hope it is that. I meant it to be. A plain word is a dreadful thing."

"You will take the legacy, and do what it in effect forbids?"

"I said it was dreadful," said Hugo.

"Then there is no more to be said."

"That is a relief, Ninian."

"Your mother must have known it might work out like this, Ninian," said Teresa.

"She added the message to ensure that it did not."

"Hugo was to have the money in any case," said Egbert.

"Money! She felt there were other things. It made her think too well of other people."

"She did not do that," said Teresa with a smile.

"In this case we must feel she did."

"So there was someone who thought better of me than I deserved," said Hugo. "It is a thing I did not expect to say."

"It is not the one I would choose at this moment," said Ninian.

"Well, that is fortunate, as you could not say it. She thought the same of you as you deserved."

"My dear mother! There was nothing false between us. As there now is between you and her."

164

"And between you and me, Ninian. And if you are not careful, there will cease to be."

Ninian turned to his daughter and spoke as if in sudden recollection.

"I have been wondering whether to put a memorial tablet to your grandmother in the church. Do you feel she would wish it?"

"She did not think of it. I hardly see what it would do for her."

"It would not do anything for you? You do not feel her life should be commemorated? You would not have felt it?"

"We should put up so many memorials, if we considered our personal feelings. People are usually commemorated for some public service."

"And the years of personal service do not count?"

"Only to us. It was to us that it was given."

"It is we who should place the memorial."

"Well, so it is, Father. And it could do no harm."

"That is hardly a ground for the time and trouble and cost."

"Well, that is what I thought."

"Would you always have thought it? Would you always have been dry and logical and without larger impulse? Is it the new interest in legacies and kindred things? Has there come to be nothing else?"

"Those are in our minds at the moment. You are glad of your own share."

"Not for my own sake. But let her be glad of them for hers, if they are her concern now," said Ninian, as he turned away. "Let her leave the deeper things. Perhaps they have been too deep. We may not have known her."

"She can hear no more," said Teresa. "No one else would have heard so much. It does harm and will leave a memory."

"If you are equal to it, Egbert," said Ninian, turning to his son, "we might go and review the new position. I

165

would not suggest it to-day, but this talk has taken our minds from their natural course, and made it hardly fitting to return to it."

"We have had enough of it all," said his wife. "We will go out of doors and forget it. Your feelings need a rest, and not only yours."

Ninian laid his hand on Egbert's shoulder, paused for the women to precede him, glanced at his daughter as she waited for Hugo, and went from the house.

"Lavinia, what can be done? Shall we always be in his power? Will he always have it all?"

"Yes, always most of it. We could never cast him off."

"I will say the truth. I think I could. He does all he can to help us. We will live at a distance from him."

"No, I must be near him. I can't help my feeling. I have tried to lose it and I have lost a part. But something remains and holds me to him. To give it up would tear up the roots of my life."

"I have never believed in God. I believe in him now. We have known he is a father. And I see that he is yours. There are the anger, jealousy, vaingloriousness, vengefulness, love, compassion, infinite power. The matter is in no doubt."

"If simplicity is our object, here is our scene," said Ninian in a cold tone, as they approached the garden assigned to the children. "Let us see what is taking place."

Leah was holding a tombstone in position, while Hengist piled up some earth to keep it secure. Agnes lay on the grass at hand, writing with a preoccupied expression.

"What are you doing?" said Ninian. "Where did you get the stone?"

"From the back of the churchyard," said his son. "We are putting up a monument to Grandma. It is quite proper, as the tombstone is a real one. The words are worn away, and Agnes is writing some more."

"It will be a sacred spot. People have more honour when

they are dead," said Leah, who perhaps gave her own support to the theory.

"It will be sacred to me," said Ninian, turning to retrace his steps to the house.—"Now how our minds work on similar lines, when they are bound by affection and sympathy! The idea of my mother's passing without visible remembrance was unnatural to them, as it was to me. They are at a stage when the first true instincts have not been blunted."

"And are you still at the stage?" said Hugo.

"Yes, as regards my mother. I hope I shall always be. I wonder you do not feel more of a son to her."

"I do feel one. She has given me reason."

"I was not thinking of the legacy."

"Neither was Hugo," said Lavinia.

"Well I was. I do like to dwell on it. It improves me so much. Something of bitterness seems to melt away."

"It is a strange thing," said Ninian, almost with a smile. "But we do not accept change. It sometimes goes too deep. I almost found myself saying I must go to my mother."

"Suppose you had quite said it?" said Hugo. "What should we have done?"

"You do not know?" said Ninian. "Lavinia would once have known."

"It is true that I do not know now, Father."

"I know," said Teresa. "We should have waited for you to realise your mistake. And that would have been in a moment."

"I could never have done any more," said Lavinia.

"I should have been at a loss," said Hugo. "But I don't see how anyone could have known."

"It would have been clear to me," said Ninian.

"You are trying to be subtle. And I almost think you are succeeding."

"You do not emulate me? You are open and simple in your outlook on your life."

"Not more than the rest of us," said Lavinia.

"Come, you have not found that," said Ninian. "Have you forgotten your grandmother?"

"No, I remember her, and everything about her. It is you who are beginning to forget."

"Why do you want to be estranged from me, my child? In order to marry against my will without compunction?"

"We shall both do that," said Hugo. "And quite without it. And you are taking your own way to the estrangement."

"And a sure one," said Teresa.

"There is no way," said Ninian.

"I hardly think there is," said Lavinia, almost wearily. "If there was, it would have been found by now."

"Would you like to see my mother's will, Hugo?" said Ninian. "And her message to you at the end?"

"No, I should find it too much. Such things go very deep with me."

"Would anyone of whom that was true, say it?"

"I thought you did not know, Ninian. You did not mean to make a heartless suggestion."

"I think I should show you the message. She meant you to see it."

"But must not time elapse, before I face the familiar hand?"

"So you really find it a subject for jest?"

"It is my way of steeling myself against it. In these matters we are always misunderstood."

Ninian left them and returned with the will, laid it on the library table and stood aside. For a time no one moved or spoke. Then Hugo went up and looked at it.

"Well?" said Ninian, after a pause.

"Well, it is just as you said it was."

"You see it with your own eyes now?"

"I had seen it through yours. You had the power to bring it before me."

"You can see my mother forcing herself to form the words."

"Oh, no, I cannot. It would be too much."

"The writing wrung my heart," said Ninian.

"Why did you ask me to see it? So that my heart would be wrung?"

"I hoped it would be touched enough for the words to ∴ their work."

"Why only touched, when yours was wrung?"

"My words were the right ones," said Ninian, and left the room.

He came on the children returning from the garden.

"Well, is the memorial complete?"

"We couldn't make it stand," said Hengist. "And Agnes made the epitaph just from herself and not from all of us."

"Is there any need to have one?"

"Yes, or it would be a memorial to someone else."

"Who had no name," said Leah, "and only lived nineteen years."

"That disposes of the matter. Is not Miss Starkie with you to-day?"

"No, it is her free afternoon. Grandma used to wonder why she wanted one."

"To have a respite from the three of you. I do not share the wonder."

"I daresay her life does need courage," said Agnes, lifting her brows.

"Well, run upstairs and behave as if she was with you."

"Nurse will be there," said Leah. "We can't be left alone. It has been proved."

"You turn your eyes on yourselves. I hope you are pleased with what you see."

The children laughed and ran to the stairs, Agnes chancing to drop a piece of paper as she went. Ninian picked it up.

'In memory of Selina, beloved and loving grandmother of Agnes Middleton, who died on the——'

His daughter paused and turned, and he let the paper fall and re-entered the library.

"Should not Hugo and Lavinia sometimes be left to themselves?" he said in a cold tone. "If their relation is accepted, it should be observed. Are you not too often with them?"

His wife and son rose and followed him, and the two were alone.

"So we shall never be forgiven," said Lavinia. "It will work itself into our lives."

"Further into his. He is planning it himself. He will lose the most."

"I believe he is trying to serve me. He is honest in part of what he says."

"What right has he to judge? Has he used you so well? You have not thought so. And I have always been with you. Always, as you remember."

"At the time of the letter do you mean?"

"Well, at all times."

"I think you loved the sinner and hated the sin."

"I could hate nothing of yours. In any place of yours I see myself. But we who have had nothing, want the most. We know what it is to be without. And it has all to be put into so short a time. You may be right in what you say. Your father sees a part of the truth."

CHAPTER XIII

"Egbert, I shall never say it," said Hugo. "You would not believe me, if I did. It may be no good to try."

"If you mean me to believe it, you can do your best."

"Tell me the most unlikely thing you can think of."

"That Father will make over everything to me. That you will marry Miss Starkie. That he will countenance your marrying Lavinia. That you will give up the idea."

"Say no more, Egbert."

"What do you mean? What is it?"

"What you have said. You see I could not say it."

"You are not going to marry Lavinia! Has she changed her mind?"

"Well, she does not know about it. People do not know their own minds. You will bring her to the knowledge."

"You have changed yours? What are you trying to say?"

"I have tried in vain. The words will not pass my lips. I can't forget that you will hear them."

"Say what you have to. I am waiting to hear."

"Egbert, a note of reproach is creeping into my tone. Is it like you to make things harder for me? And you did not wish me to be nearer to you. I could not feel I had a true welcome."

"That may be so. But it is another matter. Tell the simple truth."

"Well, I cannot bear to be a son to your father. Or bear Lavinia to be a daughter to him. It would keep me in his power. And I have the chance to escape. Your grandmother was a great woman. I should like to be Dickens, so that I could be unrestrained about her."

"What would he say about Lavinia?"

"That she had come to know her own heart, and feel her father came first to her."

"Have you no deeper reason?"

"Yes, but it is difficult to make it sound deep. I want to feel my independence and indulge my selfish, bachelor tastes. I don't think it does sound so. You would never believe how deep it is. Perhaps you have not sounded my depths."

"Have you spoken to Lavinia?"

"No, of course I have not. It would be behaving like a man. She will speak to me through you."

"You will speak for yourself. It is time you did behave like one."

"Egbert, it is a thing I have never done. And no one could do it without practice. You are experienced in what you have to do. You know you have done it many times. You did not want me as a brother."

"I find I want you less in your present character."

"Well, you will be rid of me. You will speak to your sister about being wise while there is time. What has been done can be done again."

"She would not listen to me. The result is always the same."

"Egbert, have you been disloyal to me? I think you owe me some amends."

"You owe this to yourself."

"Why do we owe such things to ourselves? Restitution and confession and others of the kind? They are what we owe to other people. I owe myself some ease and freedom before it is too late. You must see it is late enough. No doubt you despise me for it."

"Are you wasting your pathos on me?"

"You know that nothing should be wasted. You must let it do its work."

"Have you lost your feeling for Lavinia?"

"No, but I have so much for myself. Even more than I knew. And I have such a small nature. I should be jealous of her father and of Teresa and of you. And how could I be a husband? He has to be the mainstay of a household."

"You must have seen yourself as one."

"No, I saw myself escaping with Lavinia. And the thought filled my mind to the exclusion of any other. So that is a thing that can happen."

"And the thought failed to hold its place?"

"I can say nothing. I know it is just. And I don't expect justice tempered with mercy. I have only seen that mercy is tempered with justice. I think people get confused."

"I don't understand the sudden change."

"It is too bad to be understood. It has come from my having more money. Let your thoughts shy away from it. It is what I do."

"So you have done what Grandma wanted."

"Yes, it was the least I could do for her. Her last wish is fulfilled. If only she could know!"

"It seems that she did. Well, the change may be for the best. But Lavinia is not prepared."

"It is in your hands. And how fortunate that is! Suppose it was in your father's!"

"I wonder you can ask me to do such a thing."

"It is all I can do. I cannot force you to it. But I know you will not fail me. And I shall not get off unscathed. Your father will not hide his happiness. He will not even try to. That will be my punishment, and a very real one I shall find it. I feel as if I were reading aloud."

"I wish you were. This business is not imaginary."

"Egbert, through it all I am glad for you. But I hope it will not draw you closer to your father. I shall have been punished enough."

"He and I will be of one mind. I do not deny it."

"I hope the old days will not return for him. My punishment would be almost greater than I could bear."

"I have no pity for you. You are thinking of yourself."

"I wonder why that sounds so bad. It is the usual thing.

I think it is the only thing. I have never met any other. It is what I am asking of you now. If you will not do it, things must remain as they are."

"You mean you will marry Lavinia?"

"What can I do, if you will not think of yourself? That is too rare a thing for me to deal with. I have no understanding of it."

"Well, it seems I must do what I can."

"You will succeed. People do, when they are thinking of themselves. That is why everyone is so successful. I have heard of failures, but I cannot think of any. I see that thinking of other people might lead to them."

"How have you seen yourself?"

"I do not look at myself. I have not dared. They say there are things worse than an honest failure. And I suppose I must be one of them."

Egbert turned away in silence and went to seek his sister. There was more risk than use in delay. He found her in the library, and spoke as he knew he must.

"Lavinia, there is a word I must say again. I have said it many times. This will have to be the last."

"It will. The time is short. Is there any need to say it?"

"Yes, I feel there is. What are you to have for what you give? For what you give up? Is Hugo even giving you all he has? And he has so much less than you."

"What has he, that he is not giving?"

"There is one thing that is our own. Our aloofness and life within ourselves. His will hold him apart. And now his independence will support it. I feel you have not seen the truth."

"I feel you have not. Truth is deeper than you know."

Egbert was silent, and his sister suddenly sent her eyes over his face.

"So that is what it is! I felt something in him. That is what it was. There was something different. So nothing is what we think it is. This has not been what I thought."

"You know it in time. No harm is done. It might have been too late."

There was a pause.

"Yes, harm is done. I am wiser, and that comes from harm. We don't hear it comes from happiness. 'Sadder and wiser' is what we say. In a real sense it is too late. Well, everything is at an end. The future is changed in a moment. You did not think it would be so easy. I should not have thought it would. But what did he say? Not the things you have said?"

"It is for you to say the word to him."

"Yes, it is from me it must come. Anything else would harm us both. And I begin to feel it has always been there and unsaid. That is the thing that can hardly be helped. But we will not say so, as it has not been said. I think I shall be glad it has not. Yes, take the word to him from me. He has chosen to hear it from you. And there is no one else. Father would like to say it, but he would like it too much."

"What would Father like too much?" said Ninian, as he passed through the room. "There is little he can like at all in these days."

"Telling Hugo that he and I will not be married," said Lavinia in a clear tone. "It is late to make the change, but it comes in time. You and Grandma and Egbert were wise. But I don't want to hear any self-praise. I should take the current view of it."

"My dear one, it is praise of you that we should hear," said Ninian, coming forward. "You show yourself indeed. The self your father has seen in you. We are not to lose you. The shadow is lifted from the future. The true light is shed. How much you and I will do with our forces joined! I hope Hugo does not make it hard for you?"

"I am to tell him for her," said Egbert. "There are reasons why that is best."

"As she will. It is for her to say. And for you to help her, as you always have. And a thing that has to be done, is better done soon. It will be well to get it behind."

Egbert smiled at his father's tone and suppressed any impulse to delay. He returned to Hugo and waited until he spoke.

"Is this the eternal silence? That comes to us all in the end?"

"It is certainly a long one," said Egbert.

"Pray do not speak to me in a distant tone. You know what I am steeling myself to face. I cannot believe I am asking the question. But what did Lavinia say?"

"What we knew she would. That she would break off everything and forget it. And be to you as she was before. She came to the decision at once."

"Egbert, I hope you did not misrepresent me?"

"No, I am sure I did not."

"Did she express any regret that she was not to spend her life with me?"

"No, she did not speak of it."

"And you expressed none that I was not to be your brother?"

"No, I wanted no sympathy."

"You are both your father's children. I can only find it a shock. It is not what I have thought."

"We were not as bad as he was," said Egbert, smiling at last. "He came out as himself."

"He surely hid his feelings?"

"No, he exhibited them. And they were of a definite kind. You do not need to ask what they were."

"And he might have had the authority of a father! I wonder I ever faced it. It was for Lavinia's sake. I would have done more than that for her."

"Go and meet her in an easy spirit. That is what you can do for her now. Father is with her, in a panic lest the matter be delayed. Go and put him out of his suspense."

"But this is almost too much for me. I am not a generous enemy. Enmity in me has nothing generous about it. But I suppose I am not an enemy, now I am not to be his son.

I shall be his friend again, almost his brother. I have to be very adaptable. I hardly know what I am."

They went to the library, and Hugo did not delay.

"Lavinia, you did your best. You tried to see me as worthy of you. I shall always remember your courage. I will not appeal to pity. That is a thing I have never been without. But there is something you can do for me. Do not allow your father to refer to me as your uncle. Things can carry their own sting."

"Then *Hugo* to both of us," said Ninian, in an almost genial tone. "*Hugo* to all of us here. *Uncle* only to the children."

"So there will be a sign of what is past. One little proof that it existed. It will have to be my stay."

"Well, now, you will be wanting a change," said Ninian. "One change must lead to others. And now you can do as you will."

"Why should I want one? Surely this one is enough. My place amongst you is what remains to me. Would you take from me what I have left?"

"So you are remaining in the family?"

"Ninian, have you no welcome for me? The old days are to return. I am to be an unchosen, single man, the character in which I have not failed. And now I can afford to be it. It is odd that it takes so much to be so little."

Lavinia moved to the door, and Ninian went with her, seeming to guard against anyone else's following. In the hall he paused and turned towards her.

"Well, now I must save you everything. You have faced enough. Our resources can be joined to ease your way. I have always seen it as best. It will be a simple transition, and will be made simple for you. You can put all such things from your mind."

"I have thought of them, as you have, Father. They are not nothing to me. They can be as my uncle would have left them, if he had been alone. I will transfer half the money to you, and you can use the rest for the time. I mean the interest on it, as long as I am with you."

"Does she mean that? The interest and for the time! Is that how she has come to think? No, I don't feel it is. It will go with what has gone."

"We cannot look forward. This change may foreshadow others. It shows there is a future. If I am favoured above my family, I am only glad of it. I am not different from other people. I don't know why it was thought I was. I am not sorry that I am myself."

"And neither am I," said her father, after a pause. "It is a normal, healthy self, and puts me at ease about you. If you were different from other people, there might be the other difference. Perhaps I have been afraid of it. I have no fear now."

"I don't want you to have it, Father. I have no wish to be a person apart. And I am giving up half of what is mine. My thinking of that and saying it shows how little apart I am."

"So it does. You are my honest, ordinary girl. I must be grateful for you, and not put you too high. If I have done so, I must forget it."

"You forgot it, Father. Some time ago and easily. We do not all forget. There again I prove I am not apart."

Ninian smiled and moved to the stairs, and they mounted them together. Lavinia left him and entered her room, and went on to the schoolroom.

"I have brought you some news. Lavinia is not to leave us. She is not going to be married. What do you say to it?"

There was a pause.

"It is really something less than news," said Leah.

"I could not have better, Mr. Middleton," said Miss Starkie. "I will ask no questions. I can guess how it was. Lavinia faced the truth. How I trusted she would have the courage!"

"It did not fail her. I think it could not. And her brother

came to her help. Those two are sure of each other. And so we are not to lose her. Surely that is news."

"We should not have lost her," said Agnes. "We were often to go to her house. And now she is not to have one."

"She will share this one with me. We shall do a great deal together."

"She has always shared it," said Leah. "Didn't Uncle Hugo want to marry her?"

"You know he did. The change has come from her. She felt it was wise to make it. And she knew it was my wish."

"She knew that all the time. It must have been something different."

"It takes two to make a quarrel," said Hengist. "I suppose that is what it was."

"You are wrong," said Ninian. "They will always be good friends."

"But they always are," said Leah. "This not news. It is nothing."

"It is not to me. And so it should not be to you."

"Were you jealous of Uncle Hugo?" said Hengist.

"Yes, of course I was," said his father, in a bantering tone. "She tried to like another middle-aged man better than me. I am glad she did not succeed. And now she is glad too."

"I wonder if she really is," said Agnes. "People sometimes have to pretend to be."

"What do you know about it? Well, I am surprised. I thought you would be glad to keep your sister."

"We oughtn't to be glad, unless she is," said Leah. "I mean in her heart."

"Do you not hear what I say?" said her father.

"It might not be true," said Hengist. "You have to put her in a proper light."

"My words are always true," said Ninian, going to the door. "And I hope yours are, or will be when you are older."

179

"Now I was not proud of you," said Miss Starkie.

"You always say that," said Leah.

"Well, you should give me reason for pride."

"Did you ever hope Uncle Hugo would marry you?" said Hengist, without regard to the advice. "You are about the right age."

"Well, I am some years younger. No, of course I did not hope it."

"Did you feel he was too far above you?"

"In what way?" said Miss Starkie.

"In the ordinary ways. He would not have been a governess, if he had been a woman."

"It might not have been so unlikely, if he had had the education."

"Perhaps he did aspire to her hand," said Leah.

"What is the jest?" said Hugo, opening the door.

"A jest indeed, Mr. Hugo. Almost too simple to be called one. Something it would be foolish to repeat."

"That you should marry *her*, as you are not to marry Lavinia," said Hengist.

"*She* would not accept me. I am not cultured enough."

"That is what she said," said Leah.

"Indeed it is not, Mr. Hugo. It did not come in like that. It is a most misleading thing to say. They were talking nonsense, and I fell in with it to save trouble."

"That is what I am doing."

"You are the right age for her," said Hengist.

"No, I am too old."

"She said that too," said Leah.

Miss Starkie raised her eyes and shoulders and did no more.

"Then of course you are too old for Lavinia," said Hengist.

"Yes, it is agreed that I am."

"We do not talk about age," said Miss Starkie. "I shall have to forbid you to speak."

"She hasn't as much power as that," said Hengist.

"You know her power is absolute," said Hugo.

"Then she could have married you, if she liked. It shows she didn't want to."

"Do you feel you have had an escape?" said Leah.

"I must congratulate you, Mr. Hugo," said Miss Starkie, with the suitable expression.

"Does she feel there are veiled insults in our words?" said Leah.

"Nothing you say is veiled," said Miss Starkie. "It is all very open and obvious."

"There is an insult that is not veiled," said Hugo.

"Ought she to insult us?" said Hengist.

"I am always one by myself, Uncle," said Agnes. "I shall be lonely without Grandma."

"Yes. So will many of us."

"She won't be," said Hengist, indicating Miss Starkie. "She used to be disparaging about her."

"Now how is anyone to understand you?" said Miss Starkie, naturally above other people in this line.

"Grandma said things she wasn't meant to hear, when she could hear them," said Leah, in explanation to Hugo. "She always said she was not herself, when she said them."

"Now if your uncle knows what you mean, I do not. And I had many talks with your grandmother when she was herself."

"When did you have them?" said Hengist.

"Not when you were there," said Miss Starkie, with a truth that might have been given a wider sphere.

"I like to remember what Grandma said about me," said Agnes.

"Yes, Agnes. It is a memory to carry with you."

"Do you carry your memory?" said Hengist.

"Yes, that of a personality it could be a privilege to meet."

"But wasn't one to her," said Leah. "I don't suppose she would have them."

"What privileges have you?" said Hugo.

"We haven't any. We are not ashamed of it. It is not our fault."

"You may not know what privileges are," said Miss Starkie. "Everyone does not recognise them."

"Father has the most," said Hengist. "Too many for one person."

"He has proportionate responsibilities."

"They can be privileges," said Agnes.

"He has Lavinia again now," said Leah.

"Yes, I had to let him have her," said Hugo. "It is to him that she belongs."

"You exercised a privilege, Mr. Hugo," said Miss Starkie.

Hugo left them and went downstairs, and on the way met Ninian. The latter had entered the library unheard, and silently withdrawn. His wife and son and daughter were talking by the fire, and Hugo's chair awaited him.

"The family expects you, Hugo. You were right to feel you belonged to it. I am going upstairs for a while. I will come down when the tea goes in."

At this hour Ainger bore the tray across the hall, accompanied or rather attended by James, and with the accustomed figure in the background.

"So nothing is to happen, Cook. It seems a house where nothing can."

"If that is your choice of expression."

"Well, how would you put it?"

"A Hand has intervened. And a state of things is restored."

"James!" said Ainger, indicating something on the floor.

"Yes, sir," said James, as he sprang to retrieve it.

"An improvement, Cook," said Ainger, turning his thumb towards his assistant.

"A thing that might take place in more than one of us."

"Is there room for it in you?"

"It is not my habit to refer to myself," said Cook, who had not broken it.

"Well, there is only dullness in front of us."

"That may be in ourselves, Ainger. And what is your right to variety? How do you regard yourself?"

"As someone whose claims are passed over."

"It might be inferred that they are absent in your case."

"I am not dull," said James, standing upright with a satisfied expression.

"It is a wise word, James, and may lead to bettering yourself."

"Till I am like Mr. Ainger," said James, in deep agreement.

"He is born to be a slave," said Ainger, who perhaps hardly opposed the tendency.

"To render service," said Cook, glancing at James.

"I was not born to it," said the latter, in honest admission. "But I am one who learns."

"No more trouble with the name, Cook. That is in the past."

"*James* is a usual name for a house servant," said the new owner of it with fluency. "And it saves inconvenience."

"Saves whom?" said Ainger. "Those who have the least?"

"They should not have any," said James, in a grave tone.

"So one of them thinks he is having it now," said Ainger, glancing up the stairs.

"My bell, sir," said James, leaping towards them.

"Why can't they keep together and save people's legs?" said Ainger, caressing one of his own.

"We need not enquire into reasons. They are entitled to them."

"The master will have tea in his room," said James, returning equipped with a tray.

"Then you can toil up with it," said Ainger, as he supplied what was needed.

James held the tray before him, and mounted the stairs with a swift, light tread.

"The new generation cometh," said Ainger, "and might as well be the old."

"Well, all things need not pass away."

"Some of them should. Some people are put too high. They fail in their own sphere. The master and Miss Lavinia; the old master and Mr. Hugo; and the old mistress in a way. Ah, I have heard, and said to myself: 'How are the mighty fallen!'"

"You need not say it to anyone else. And where is the call to confer with yourself? Everyone is not mighty. We can think of instances."

"Some more hot water in five minutes," said James, running noiselessly down the stairs.

"So he feels he is still mighty," said Ainger, as he took the jug. "The very minutes stipulated!"

VIRAGO MODERN CLASSICS

The first Virago Modern Classic, *Frost in May* by Antonia White, was published in 1978. It launched a list dedicated to the celebration of women writers and to the rediscovery and reprinting of their works. Its aim was, and is, to demonstrate the existence of a female tradition in fiction which is both enriching and enjoyable. The Leavisite notion of the 'Great Tradition', and the narrow, academic definition of a 'classic', has meant the neglect of a large number of interesting secondary works of fiction. In calling the series 'Modern Classics' we do not necessarily mean 'great' — although this is often the case. Published with new critical and biographical introductions, books are chosen for many reasons: sometimes for their importance in literary history; sometimes because they illuminate particular aspects of womens' lives, both personal and public. They may be classics of comedy or storytelling; their interest can be historical, feminist, political or literary.

Initially the Virago Modern Classics concentrated on English novels and short stories published in the early decades of this century. As the series has grown it has broadened to include works of fiction from different centuries, different countries, cultures and literary traditions. In 1984 the Victorian Classics were launched; there are separate lists of Irish, Scottish, European, American, Australian and other English speaking countries; there are books written by Black women, by Catholic and Jewish women, and a few relevant novels by men. There is, too, a companion series of Non-Fiction Classics constituting biography, autobiography, travel, journalism, essays, poetry, letters and diaries.

By the end of 1990 over 350 titles will have been published in these two series, many of which have been suggested by our readers.

Also by Ivy Compton-Burnett

TWO WORLDS AND THEIR WAYS

Sefton and his sister Clemence are dispatched to separate boarding schools. Their father's second marriage, their mother's economies, provide perfect opportunities for mockery, and home becomes a source of shame. More wretched is their mother's insistence that they excel. Their desperate means to please her incite adult opprobrium, but how did the children learn to deceive? Here staccato dialogue, brittle aphorisms and an excoriating wit are used to unparalleled and subversive effect ruthlessly to expose the wounds beneath the surface of family life.

'Probably the purest and most original of contempory English artists' – *Rosamond Lehmann*

'She saw life in terms of Greek tragedy, its cruelties, ironies – above all its passions ' – *Anthony Powell*

Also of interest

A PARTICULAR PLACE
By Mary Hocking

In this, her most memorable and triumphant novel to date, Mary Hocking is confirmed as the successor to Elizabeth Taylor and Barbara Pym.

The parishioners of a small West Country market town are uncertain what to make of their new Anglican vicar with his candelit processions. And, though Micheal Hoath embraces challenge, his enthusiasm is sapped by their dogged traditionalism. Moreover, Valentine's imperial temperament is more suited to the amateur dramatics she excels at than the role of vicar's wife. Their separate claims to insecurity are, for the most part, concealed and so both are surprised when Michael falls in love with a member of his congregation: a married women, neither young nor beautiful. In tracing the effects of this unlikely attraction, Mary Hocking offers humour, sympathy and an overwhelming sense of the poignancy of human expectations.

'Mary Hocking's wry straightness makes posher novels about marital unfaithfulness seem arch, pretentious and overdone by comparison' – *Observer*

'Mary Hocking is an undisguised blessing' – *Christopher Wordsworth, Guardian*

HESTER LILLY
By Elizabeth Taylor

Muriel, the elegant wife of a conscientious headmaster, fears the arrival of his orphaned cousin, Hester Lilly, though when she meets her, Muriel experiences a sensation of relief. How can someone so ill put-together pose a threat to her carefully nurtured marriage? But Muriel is quite misled: almost before she knows it she is locked into a desperate struggle with the waif-like Hester Lilly. In this her first collection of short stories (1954), Elizabeth Taylor beautifully charts the territory that so much became hers. Here we also encounter the poignant, muted agony of long marriages; the frittering away of lives in the polite English countryside; the oddity and freshness of children's vision in opposition to the adult world, and much else besides. These tales are superb examples of Elizabeth Taylor's art.

Her genius – and this is a just word – lies in her discriminating observations of the exact comment' – *Marghanita Laski*

'Perceptive, ironic, accomplished. She is a genuinely creative writer' – *The Times*